By SHAY HUNTER

Tranny

911

COMP
SER

Library of Congress Control Number: 2013940145

ISBN 10: 0989084558
ISBN 13: 978-0989084550

Cover Design: Davida Baldwin www.oddballdsgn.com
Editor: Advanced Editorial Services
Graphics: Davida Baldwin
www.thecartelpublications.com
First Edition

Printed in the United States of America

THIS NOVEL IS A PART OF

THE CARTEL PUBLICATIONS

A SUBSIDIARY OF
THE CARTEL PUBLICATIONS

CHECK OUT OTHER TITLES BY THE CARTEL PUBLICATIONS

WWW.THECARTELPUBLICATIONS.COM

What's Poppin' Fam,

At the end of the year in 2012, T. Styles and I came together in one of our many meetings, and decided that in 2013, we would do everything possible to meet ALL of our deadlines.

We have kept our word to ensure that our customers receive the most original novels, based on the publication dates. We are extremely proud, and our customers have also expressed their appreciation. With at least two novels a month hitting the shelves, this is not always easy, but we have made it possible. So thank you for riding with us.

Now, onto "Tranny 911". Shay Hunter's debut novel is crazy. With all the news surrounding illegal body enhancing injections, this novel comes right on time. Although this book is entertainment, some of the details within its pages contain procedures that should not be attempted. There are people all over the world who have lost their lives trying to illegally alter their bodies, so please read it for what it is, entertainment, pure and simple!

Keeping in line with tradition, we want to give respect to a trailblazer paving the way. With that said we would like to recognize:

Don Miguel Ruiz is the author of the novel, "The Four

Agreements". This book teaches that by following the four agreements, positive changes will occur in your life, giving you personal freedom. We highly recommend this novel to serve as food for the heart and soul.

Get to it! I'll see you in the next novel.

Be Easy!
Charisse "C. Wash" Washington
Vice President
The Cartel Publications
www.thecartelpublications.com

www.twitter.com/cartelbooks

www.facebook.com/cartelpublications

Note to Readers

During your read of "Tranny 911" please keep in mind that the characters often refer to themselves as women because in their heart and mind they are. Please don't get confused during the duration of the storyline by the use of exchanging feminine to masculine references.

Prologue

As the melody of crickets chirped within the darkness of Washington D.C's toughest neighborhood, a thug name Mirando sat on the steps of a brick building, eyeing two friends walking towards a party. Although both of them were sexy, it was Charles Monroe, with his angelic face, curvy body and outrageous sex appeal that caused Mirando's manhood to stiffen.

"Don't worry about anything, Sherry, trust me, he's going to love you," Charlie said, as he walked arm and arm down the block with her. "You always worrying about things when you don't have to. Shit, you may find out when you get there that he likes you too."

"It's easy for you to say," Sherry said, looking into Charles' hazel eyes. "I mean look at you. You're a boy and you're more beautiful than I am. I hate to

even walk with you down the street sometimes," she giggled.

Although her comment was geared as a compliment, Charles suddenly felt less than. He didn't want to be a beautiful boy, he wanted to be a woman, and he did everything he could to change himself. He wore makeup when he was out of the house. He slid into the tightest pants he could find at all times, and he eliminated the base in his voice. Through it all, he never felt like who he really was, a woman. Unless he was having sex with a man.

"How can I be more beautiful than you?" he said as they approached the brick building, which was to play host to the party. "You are a girl. The only thing I can do is pretend, until I have enough money to do something about it. Sometimes I wonder why God did this to me."

She stopped walking and looked into his eyes. "You talk like that but you can't be serious."

"What you mean?"

"Come on, Charles, tell the truth, you know you beautiful." She rubbed her soft hand down his cheekbone. "With a face like yours you have to know you got it going on. Women would kill for those long eyelashes, those brown eyes and that cute little button nose."

"You say stuff like that all the time, but I really don't think I'm beautiful. I mean I'll probably never have long flowing hair. Or hips and breasts like *yours." He sighed. "I'm going to always be a boy who will grow up to be a man, who just so happens to be gay."*

"Charles, stop talking like that. You know how many procedures there are today? For the right money you can do anything you want. It's just about raising the funds...you know that already. And this hair, come on girl, you know you can buy it!"

"That's right, for the right money. Don't forget that I'm broke and living with my father right now. He doesn't want to give me money for lunch let alone the coins for my procedure."

"Then you'll have to raise your own money, and I'll help you. Besides, this is your last year in high school. Next year you can get a job and—"

"Damn, shorty, you phat as shit," Joshua from up the block yelled behind Charles. But when Charles turned around and he saw the person he was lusting after was a boy, he felt disgusted and humiliated at the same time. He backed away from Charles and clenched his fists. He felt like he tricked him.

"Damn, homie, let me find out you like them boys," his friend Nick joked. "You know I always thought you was a little sweet around the edges," dude continued pinching his face.

"Nigga, get the fuck off of me 'fore I break your jaw." Nick backed down and Joshua looked at Charles. "Fucking faggies, always trying to confuse

a nigga and shit." He walked into the party with his crew feeling disgusted the entire way.

Charles' body drooped after Joshua's rough words.

"Charles, don't worry about him," Sherry said softly. She wiggled her arm through his and escorted him into the party. "We are going to have a ball to-night I don't care what nobody got to say." When he didn't seem upbeat she said, "Charlie, have fun for me. Please."

He removed his gaze from the ground and looked into her eyes. "Okay"—

He smiled— "I'll do it for you, but I'm going to need something to drink, to relax my mind."

Once inside the party, they were overcome by the thick crowd. The heat rising off of the bodies of the teenagers caused the temperature to swelter and the windows to sweat. Music pumped from a floor speaker, rattling the family pictures on the wall.

"It's hot as shit in here," Sherry said wiping sweat off of her face. "They should open up the win-dows or something. Maybe they trying to blow nig-gas out."

"Maybe we should go, Sherry," Charles re-plied. Truthfully he was still uneasy about how Josh-ua treated him and he wanted to bounce. "I don't feel comfortable here."

"Charlie, don't let that nigga ruin your night. Let's go get something to drink so you can relax a

little, before you know it you'll not even remember him."

They walked over to the table, grabbed two cups of spiked punch, and found an empty portion against the wall to lean against. It was people watching time.

It wasn't long before Bernard Shane, the 21-year old man of Sherry's dreams, walked into the party with two of his friends.

Sherry yanked Charles arm, causing him to drop his cup to the floor. "Oh my, god, Sherry? Why you do that, girl? They gonna flip when they see this stain on the carpet."

"There's going to be more stains than that on the floor after this ghetto ass party is over." She paused. "But look"— she placed her empty cup down on the table. "There he goes right there!" she point-ed into the thickness of the party. "That's the nigga I was telling you about."

Charles excitedly scanned the crowd eager to see this man Sherry couldn't stop talking about. He was happy for her until he was staring into the eyes of the last person he had sex with. Out of all of the men in the world, she would pick one who had a thing for both men and women.

Although it was awhile back, Charles thought about the night they had sex often. He was on his way to the gym, to lose the last five pounds he gained after staying over his friend Dixon's house

*for the weekend. On his way into the gym, he ran in-
to Bernard who was sweaty and coming out after his
workout. His body seemed to sparkle under the blaz-
ing sun, and his long dreads were snatched back into
a neat ponytail. By all accounts he was beyond sexy.
The attraction was evident and when they looked at
each other, Charles felt electricity shoot through his
body. Although Charles was a teenager, and Bernard was older, Charles still wanted him.*

*"I guess you're about to get yours over with
huh?" Bernard said as his eyes rolled over Charles'
body. "Your workout that is."*

*"Yes, is it crowded?" Charles asked trying to
make small talk.*

*"Not really." He looked back at the gym, before
facing Charles again. "Although you got some fakers
in there hogging up the treadmills but you should be
good." He wiped his face with his towel. "I was just
about to grab some fish tacos from the Taco truck up
the street."*

*Charles grinned, realizing this was his queue.
He needed to either say something good, or he
would miss an opportunity to connect and get to
know Bernard a little better. "You want any company?"*

"Of course I do," Bernard grinned.

*Five minutes later Bernard was fucking him
from behind in the backseat of his silver Escalade.
Although Charles was hoping that their encounter*

would lead to something better, he was willing to take whatever he could get at the moment. But it was over as soon as it began and Charles was overwhelmed with guilt.

Bernard climbed back into the driver's seat. "So look, give me your number and I'll get up with you later." He pulled up his pants, turned the car on and put the car into drive. "I wish I could hang out but I got some things to do."

"What's up with the fish tacos? I thought we were going to grab something to eat."

"Oh...uh I can't get them." He looked at his watch. "I got some things to take care of later. Now give me your number."

"You got a pen and a paper?"

"Naw...but tell me, I'll remember it."

Charles swallowed the lump in his throat, and then rattled off his number. He knew he'd never see or hear from Bernard again, and he was right. He felt used but what could he do now? Bernard threw him out of his car, and Charles drove all the way back to the gym, with his heart in his hand. He often wondered if there was anything about him that Bernard liked, but after a few more weeks he realized it didn't matter.

"Charles, are you okay?" Sherry asked. "Why you looking all crazy and shit?"

SHAY HUNTER

"Uh...yes...I'm fine." He rubbed his eyes. *"But where is your friend again? I don't see him."* He lied.

"He's over there with the locks," she responded jumping up and down, *"you see him?"* He was hoping that she was talking about somebody else. *"Isn't he so fucking sexy?"*

Unable to break his friend's heart, Charles walked over to the punch bowl without responding. But she followed him. *"What's going on, Charles? Why you acting funny?"* He didn't respond. *"I asked what's going on? Why you acting differently? Are you ready to go or something?"*

"I don't want to talk about it right now, Sherry."

Sherry examined him thoroughly. If there was one thing about their bond it was that they had a close relationship. So the fact that he didn't respond to her crush made her uncomfortable. She played over and over in her mind what could be wrong. And then suddenly it dawned on her. She felt gut punched, because she knew exactly what was happening. *"You fucked him didn't you? You fucked Bernard?"*

"It wasn't like that," he replied softly.

"Then what was it like, Charlie?"

"Maybe he isn't gay, Sherry." He shrugged. *"Lots of guys have sex with other men but it doesn't*

mean anything. I haven't spoken to him in almost two months."

"If he fucked you, he's gay," she said, suddenly changing her mood. Her head throbbed and she was so embarrassed. "I hate you so much right now."

"Me," he pointed to himself. "What did I do?"

"You can never let me have anybody. When I wanted to be with Larry, I found out you fucked him in the boy's locker room at school. When I liked Chris, I found out you fucked him at his cousin's house after school. I mean, damn, can't I have anybody?" Tears rolled down her face and suddenly she was filled with anger for him, and he felt devastated.

Charles and Sherry had been friends all of their lives and she'd never, ever, spoken to him like this before. And judging by the hate in her voice, he could tell that she felt about him in this way for a long time.

"Sherry, I'm sorry, I really am. I didn't mean to hurt you, and I hope you believe me when I say that. I never went after those guys. They just came at me. You'd be surprised at how many guys like other men. I just—"

She frowned. "Oh so what, everybody wants you now? Everybody has to be with you? What is so irresistible about you? You not even a fucking girl. Please tell me because I gotta hear this shit!"

"I'm not saying that. I'm saying—"

SHAY HUNTER

"Fuck you, Charlie," she said. "Fuck you, Charlie Monroe!"

Sherry walked away, leaving him stuck and in the middle of the floor. He could feel the tears stream down his face, and he ran into the bathroom to get himself together.

Fifteen minutes later he was still sitting on the toilet and at least three people knocked on the door trying to get in to use the bathroom, including the person who lived there. But Charles refused to open the door.

Thirty minutes later, he threw water on his face and decided since Sherry was angry with him that he couldn't stay at the party any longer. The only reason he was there was because of her.

When he opened the door, Charles was caught off guard due to a blow to the middle of the face, courtesy of Bernard. He struck him so hard, with a closed fist, that Charles fell, and the back of his head fell against the sink, bringing it down from the wall. Instead of leaving, Bernard picked Charles up by the collar and hit him over and over in the face with his fist.

Although Charles was also male, his features were tiny and petite and not built for such abuse. First his nose fractured, then his eye blackened and his lips burst open like grapes. When Bernard was done he dropped him and looked down at his work.

"That's for lying and telling people I fucked you, nigga," he yelled pointing at him.

When Charles looked up, there was a crowd of people covering him. Sherry was by Bernard's side too, and a small hint of remorse covered her face. But nobody, not one of them, bothered to help him out.

"Now tell everybody you lied, before I murder you in here. Tell them I never touched you. Like I would fuck with another man."

Charles could feel several teeth resting on his tongue. And so much blood filled his mouth that he felt like he was about to choke. Part of him wanted to tell the world that he wasn't lying, but the other part, the human part, had a sincere desire to survive.

"I lied," he said in a low voice.

"Speak up, faggy, so that the entire party can hear you."

"I said," he swallowed. "I lied."

The crowed mumbled their disgust with Charles under their breaths.

"That's what the fuck I thought," Bernard grinned. "Now you better stay the fuck away from me. If I even see you on my side of the street, you better move to the other side.

When he was done, Bernard walked out of the bathroom and the crowd went with him. Charles lay on that floor for fifteen more minutes before Dixon came rushing inside.

SHAY HUNTER

"Oh my, god, they told me you were beat badly but I had no idea it was like this." Stronger than his years, seventeen year old Dixon lifted Charles up, and rushed him out of the party and to his house.

Thirty minutes later Dixon helped Charles walk into his apartment. But the moment the door closed behind him, Charles' father, Sam, was there waiting.

"What the fuck happened to your face?" His arms were crossed over his muscular chest.

"Some boys jumped him, Mr.—"

"Am I talking to you?" Sam pointed at Dixon's face. *"Because if I was talking to you, I would've made it clear."*

"No, sir," he said hanging his head.

"Then shut the fuck up and let the boy answer." He focused back on his son. Now…what the fuck happened to your face?"

"Somebody beat me up, because they said I lied about what we did together. It's okay, daddy. Things will be fine now."

Sam frowned, stepped back and examined his only child. The son he wanted to play ball with, talk about girls and enjoy life.

"You see what I'm saying? You'll always have problems like this, just as long as you strut around these streets like you a bitch. If your mother was

here to see this, God rest her soul"— he looked up at the cream ceiling— "she would've died all over again. Why do you have to put so much shame on us? Huh?"

"Daddy, I'm sorry, but I didn't lie. I—"

"Get out of my house, boy," he pointed at the door behind Charles. "I'm tired of looking at your face."

"Okay, daddy, I'll come back tomorrow so—"

"I don't ever want you to come back here, Charles. You aren't welcome in my home. As far as I'm concerned, I don't have any children."

"But daddy," he said with wide eyes. "I don't have anywhere else to go. What am I going to do?"

"You should've thought about that before you decided to sleep with other men. Now take your gay friend and get out of my house now! Before I dig under my couch and then you won't be able to leave." He opened the door and threw them both out.

Defeated, and barely able to see straight due to the damage Bernard caused to his face, Charles leaned against the hallway wall in his building and slid down to the floor. "I don't know where to go or what I'm going to do." He looked up at Dixon. "I'm lost."

Dixon stepped up to him. "As long as you got me, you'll always have some place to call home. That much I promise."

SHAY HUNTER

CHAPTER ONE

Charles

Five Years Later

This lady is giving me the blues right now at my job. I been on my feet for twelve hours and everything she got in her cart, I had to go get a price check on. I really just want to go home, soak my bones in my tub and go to sleep. That's the only thing about working in customer service, having to deal with people you don't like.

"Okay, ma'am, your total comes to fifty-seven dollars and thirty-three cents." I say placing her last item in her bag. "How would you like to pay for it?"

"Cash please." She pulls out a crisp one hundred dollar bill and I smile.

When I accept the money, I look at the camera on the ceiling, out of habit, and return forty-one dollars and sixty seven cents to her. Her change is a dollar short of what she is actually due, but she doesn't seem to notice as she pushes her cart out of the front door.

Since she was the one hundredth person I'd done it to today, I was going to take one hundred dollars out when my shift was over. This was smooth because unlike stealing money directly from FloorMart, I was taking money from the customers, which meant my register would never come up short.

After ringing my last customer up, I waited until the store's doors were locked. Then I opened my register and removed the cash drawer. Walking towards the back office, I quickly slide a one hundred dollar bill out of my drawer as I'm strutting down the aisle. Then I stuff it into my pocket right before I make it to the back.

The moment I stroll into the manager's office to count my cash drawer with the other employees, I notice that with the exception of a security guard, my manager, and myself we are alone. Where were all of the other employees?

I place my drawer on the table and smile at them. "Where is everybody else? I know they didn't count their drawers that fast."

"Don't worry about all of that," my manager says in a snappy tone, "take a seat, Charles."

What's wrong with her?

SHAY HUNTER

I continue to stand feeling uncomfortable. The security guard locks the door and stands behind me. My stomach rumbles and I know immediately that I have been caught.

"You look scared, Charles," she says. "Are you okay?"

"Yes, I'm fine, I just..."

My manager, Frieda Kristy, throws me disapproving looks that make me forget what I'm about to say next. She never liked me from the beginning, and since I had no other reason to go off of, I assumed it was because I was gay. I couldn't count the number of times men hit on me, and she told me over and over again that nobody would ever take me seriously. She went on to say that the only thing gay men were good for was an orgasm. It wasn't until later that I discovered from a co-worker that another man took her husband, and she hadn't been right since.

Her graying hair was pulled into a messy ponytail, and the brown glasses on her nose hung a little to the left.

"Can somebody tell me what's going on?" I look at the security guard and then back at Frieda. "I mean, should I have a lawyer?"

"I don't know, Charles. Should you?" she pauses. "Have a seat," she says again in a stern voice. "I'll make this quick."

Tranny 911

I take a seat with the assistance of the security guard's heavy press on my shoulder.

"We have been watching you for a week now, Charles," she says, "and we know that you have been shorting customers about a dollar, and taking the money for yourself."

"That's not true," I lie.

"Of course it is. Now at first, I have to admit, I didn't understand how you were stealing money, if the register was never short. It took me a moment to find out how you did it, and if you asked me it was quite brilliant. What you should have done though was quit while you were ahead."

I'm confused. Even if she knew I was shorting customers, how did she know the exact amount, simply by reviewing the cameras?

My heart pulsates in my throat, and my mind floats back to everything I did when I took the money. I was good. I was smart, and I was quick. I knew who was at work and when, and I knew who was managing the cameras and who wasn't. It was the same crew, and they did the same things everyday. So it was a wonder that we were never robbed before. How did she really find out?"

"Frieda, I think there's been a mistake I—"

My comment is butchered when she grabs the remote off of the table and points it to a TV that sits on the wall. When it brightens I see myself coming into the office just now. My long curly weave hangs

SHAY HUNTER

down my back, and my favorite silk pink shirt presents the illusion of breasts, because they are stuffed with socks. From a far I look like a girl, and I'm surprised because it's not like I see myself.

But when I focus on the real purpose of my video performance, I see me stuff the one hundred dollar bill in my blue jeans. Although the dollar amount was not visible from each customer, the money tucking was. The security guard reaches into my pocket and takes out the bill.

I was caught.

Red handed.

I didn't mean to be a thief, but I was desperate. Five years ago a man who was afraid that I would share his bisexuality with the world, assaulted me at a party. And because of it, my face was never the same. All I wanted was cosmetic surgery and later a complete sex change. As it stood I saved thirty five hundred dollars and I was a long way off from having enough. That's why I took the money everyday from work. Now I feel so dumb.

"Frieda...I...it's..."

"You're fired," she tells me with a smile. "And I want you out of here right now. You have dismantled the integrity of this organization and I will not allow it any longer."

Although I'm devastated about not having a job, I can't wait to leave, because the embarrassment is killing me. But instead of being allowed to

Tranny 911

bounce, the door opens and police officers enter the small space. I feel suffocated. I can't go home, they are taking me to jail.

"Frieda, please don't do this," I cry. "I'll pay back every penny I took. I promise."

She produces a grin, which rises slightly higher on one side of her face. "I know you're going to pay, and you're going to also be arrested. You might think you're a real woman, Charles, but you're going to a men's jail today. " She looked at the officers. "Get him out of here. Now!"

"Charles Monroe," one of the officers says as he releases a set of silver cuffs from his belt. "You are under arrest."

"Do you have any weapons on you?" a male officer asks me in the precinct.

"No," I say in a low voice.

"Speak up," he yells so loud in my face, it startles me.

"No...no, sir," I shiver. "I don't have any weapons, the other officers already patted me down."

"I didn't ask you that, I hate niggas like you," he said in a low voice that only I can hear. "You dirty fucking faggies. Pretending to be women and shit, and trying to confuse real brothers like myself.

If they could hang you all one by one, I would pay money to see that shit."

I can feel the hate spewing off of him as I recite my favorite prayer in my mind. Psalm 23.

The Lord is my shepherd I shall not want. He makes me lie down in the green pastures. He leads me beside the still waters. He restores my soul.

After the officer runs his hands over my body, he pulls the socks I have in my chest out, and throws them to the floor. And then he looks back at another officer in the room and says, "You see this shit, man? I swear this shit is getting ridiculous."

"You know the laws are changing too," the officer responds. "They can get married now. Watch out for your son."

"I wish they would try to get at my son. And I better not have one cross my path who's married either while I'm at work," he looks at me angrily again. "I'll give them something they won't be able to stand, in private."

He leads me in paths of righteousness for His name's sake.

While I'm praying, I'm suddenly yanked toward an inkpad that's sitting on a counter, where my fingers are controlled as they are pressed against it, and then a paper, which leaves my fingerprint trail. I feel humiliated. Now that I think about it, how did I ever think I'd get away with stealing from FloorMart for so long?

"Wait, man, what about that wig?" the officer in the background said. "We can't have him in there confusing the other inmates."

The officer who was processing me looked up at my hair. "Yeah, you right." He yanks my wig and exposes my brown stocking cap underneath. "That's more I like it."

Tears pour out of my eyes and I try to remain strong. *Even though I walk through the valley of the shadow of death, I fear no evil.*

I don't know if God accepts me or not, but that prayer is the only thing that kept me going for most of my life. When my father told me I couldn't come home, it kept me going. When I saw him in the street six months later, after missing him terribly, and I approached him only to be told he doesn't know me, the prayer kept me going. I'm hoping that it does it now.

"Do you want to make a call?" a woman asks me from behind.

When I wake up out of the deliberate daydream I put myself in, to avoid my current situation, I'm staring into a face of a pretty girl. She's masculine, but she places a gentle hand on my shoulder. She's what we call in the gay community as 'family' or a dominant woman.

"Yes please."

"No problem," she winks. "And don't worry about a thing, I'm here now."

SHAY HUNTER

When I look back at the officers who taunted me from the moment I got here, I notice that they are standing against the wall with attitudes. Although they give me evil looks, neither one of them bothers to say anything to me now since I'm standing with her. I guess God cares about me after all.

CHAPTER TWO

Dixie

"Bitch, you don't know what you talking about," I say to Fergie, as I nurse over tonight's dinner. "Sometimes your mouth just moves a mile a minute just so you can hear yourself talk."

I'm preparing lasagna with my homemade sauce, while shaking my tiny ass around the kitchen because the music is on. Tonight is going to be fabulous because I have so many things planned. First I'm preparing a fresh meal, second I'm expecting a boy toy to come over and play and lastly, I'm finally headlining at *Wiggles* gay club.

The thing that's spectacular about my performance is this...Wiggles doesn't allow just anybody to do their thing on the stage. Had it not been for one of the girl's cancelling, I wouldn't have gotten the call last night saying I was up. But at least I'm ready for the show.

"How the fuck you gonna tell me I don't know what I'm talking about?" Fergie says to me. "Last week and the week before that someone did *Single Ladies*. You know they hate to double dip on Beyoncé. Just do something else. It ain't like you didn't rehearse another routine. For goodness sake, Dixie, be original for once in your miserable life."

Before answering her, I stir the tomato sauce with the large spoon and taste it. It was just like I like it. So I spit in it, the way I do with all of my food when I cook. It's the one ingredient I know that even if someone tried to steal my recipe, they won't have.

"I'm not doing Lady Gaga, Ferg. I told you what I'm doing."

"Okay, well if you get down there, and they don't let you perform, I'm going to laugh my ass off. Just remember that you been warned, sweetie."

"Well knock yourself out, you were probably going to do that regardless, you hating ass bitch," I yell. "To tell you the truth it don't matter what I dance off of, when Charlie gets finished beating this face, bitch and doing this hair, they will be on their knees thanking me for showing up. From my beauty alone, trick. Please know me."

"Hold up, chile," Fergie says. "Now Ms. Charlie is a Picasso when it comes to the makeup, but even he can't perform the miracles your face needs."

"Oooo Ms. Fergie, you on fire tonight, chile." I place the sauce in the bottom of the pan, and set up the noodles for the lasagna. "What has gotten into you? You fighting with Mr. Good Dick again?"

She sighs. "That ain't even the half, but you close. This bastard gonna come over here the other day and tell me he's going back to his wife. I knew that trade was wit' his wife a long time ago, but why he cutting me off? Girl, I get tired of the games these niggas play."

"Bitch, stop!" I yell, stomping my barefoot on the kitchen floor. "Mr. Good Dick cut you off for real?" I place a layer of cheese onto the lasagna.

"I'm not even playing, Ms. Dixie, although I wish I was. You know me and that nigga been getting it in since high school. What I'm gonna do now? He's the only nigga I fucked in two years."

I bust out laughing. "Girl, it's me on this phone, not your mother. I think you got the lines crossed and forgot who you talking too. Please understand that you can keep it real with me always. With that said, you and me both know how many addresses done hosted that back pussy of yours."

"My bad," she giggles. "Well he's my favorite fuck boy. But what I'm gonna do now that he's not in my life? I know I do my thing on the side, but I thought we would always be together."

"Get you another candy man. Shit that's what we gotta do." When the line beeps I say, "Hold on girl, somebody hitting my phone." I switch over and say, "Hello there." I place the last layer of noodles over the lasagna.

"Dixie, it's me, I need your help," Charlie says in a low voice. "I know it's a bad time to be calling you, but I truly don't have a choice or no one else to call. I'm in a bind."

"Oh, my God, are you okay?" I sprinkle cheese on top of it. "You didn't get into an accident did you?"

"No, I wish I was, Dixie. I fucked up this time on a major level. You remember what I was telling you I did at the job right?"

"I do."

"Well I got arrested today."

My eyes widen and I throw the spoon into the sink. "Arrested for what?"

"For stealing from FloorMart. That's what they trying to put on me."

"Oh, Ms. Charlie," I say placing the lasagna in the oven. "I told you to be careful when you did that dumb shit. Damn!"

"I know, and I feel so badly about it too," she pauses. "Look, I know you have that show tonight, and I hate to do this to you, but I need you to come bail me out. My money is under the bed, in my shoebox."

The moment she says that, I hang up. When I do the phone rings again, and I answer it because I know Fergie was on the other line.

"Bitch, you wouldn't believe what just happened." I walk into the living room to look at the leotard I'm wearing for my performance tonight. "Please tell me why Charlie just called and said she needs me to bail her out of jail? What the fuck I look like?"

"Oh, I'm sorry, girl. You want me to do your performance tonight? I can sure use the money, because I wanted to get some injections in my ass and hips from Sugar."

"Bitch, I wish I would let you twirl on my stage," I yell. "You got me all the way fucked up. Honey, the show will go on and it will go on with me in the lead."

"Well what about Charlie? You can't leave him down there."

"I am, I can and I will. I'll pick him up after my performance. Shit, it ain't my fault he got caught stealing money from FloorMart. He needs to deal with the consequences and repercussions of his actions."

"Damn, Ms. Charlie," he says to himself. I guess he's trying to make me feel bad for him by saying his name. "I really like him, Dixie. You shouldn't leave him down there. That poor thing is all alone out in this world. If you don't get him that pretty little thing will rot!"

"The girl ain't going to die. She'll be fine until I get back. And when you think about it, she truly doesn't have a choice."

"You can be an awful person when you want to."

"Tell me something I don't know, baby love."

"You gonna pay for this, girl." She laughs. "And what did you tell him anyway?"

"I hung up in his beautiful face. And when I talk to him later I'll tell him my cell phone call dropped like I always do when I don't feel like being bothered."

"Wait, you do that shit to me all the time!"

"You are absolutely correct, just like I'm doing it to you now." I hang up on him and throw the phone in the sofa.

◀━━━◀ ◀━━━◀ ◀━━━◀

As I step off of the stage, I'm sweating and feel off balance. To make matters worse, I didn't get a dime for my performance in the wig on the stage. Whenever you perform, the queens show support by walking up to the wig and blessing it. I didn't get any money. No penny, no nickel, no nothing!

"I'm sorry, girl," one of the girls say to me when I flip my wig over to see if I have any money. "That was pretty awful to look at. Maybe you should try harder next time you think?"

"It was just like the performance you gave on Ms. Taylor Swift. And I don't know if you heard, but it wasn't nothing to look at," I say wiping sweat off of my face with a towel. "So don't come for me because I didn't send for you."

"The difference is when I stepped off of the stage I had a coin." She eyes my empty wig. "And right now your well looks a little dry."

"You know what, I don't have time for you, Belize. Miss me with all that shit."

"I'll miss you in a second, honey," she says, "right now I'm not done reading you. What's up with that face of yours?" she frowns. "I know Ms. Charlie isn't responsible for such a mess, because she's a professional. Did you call yourself doing your own makeup?" Belize walks away.

The moment she says that, I remember I left him in jail. Since I didn't make any money, and the performance didn't do what I wanted, I guess I could've scooped him up, but oh well. Hindsight is twenty-twenty.

I'm about to leave when Kenny Sugar walks his frumpy looking as up to me. Sugar is the one person who gets on my nerves. Every time he comes to me, he's asking me about Charlie. I don't trust this bitch, because for whatever reason he doesn't like me.

On several occasions I've been told that he has my name in his mouth. Like the time I got into a fight with Andre, one of the queens at the club, because he hit my car with his in the parking lot. Automatically Sugar assumed it was something I did when he didn't even know me.

"So I guess you didn't give Charlie my message. Because she hasn't called me and I refuse to believe she would do that without at least seeing what I wanted."

I sigh, and roll my eyes before batting my eyelashes. "Sugar, whatever message you gotta give Charlie you can give to me. I told you he's at work during these hours. You making the situation longer than it has to be because you're not telling me what you want with him. I'm good with relaying messages."

"Because it's none of your business."

"Okay, I guess I'll give Charlie the information when I get it."

He exhales so hard a curl on the wig I'm wearing flutters. "It's a gig for money. Are you happy now?"

This was the first time he told me what he wanted with Charlie, and I wish he had before. Because although I make a few pennies working for the government, I always welcome the opportunity to make more income.

I smile and say, "Sugar, you should've said something to me before." I giggle. "Girl, you got me yelling at you when we should be friends. I mean, why you didn't tell me that? Instead of bothering Charlie, whatever you need, I can do the job."

She shakes her head. "No, honey, I'm looking for honest queens."

I grit my teeth. "Who says I'm not honest?"

"Your actions right now prove it," she says.

"You know what, I'm not going to even argue with you. So do me a favor and just give me your number again, and I'll tell him you want him to call you."

Before he could respond I hear someone yelling in the background. "Listen up, girls," Belize says holding an upside down wig. "I need everybody to pitch in right now! Ms. Charlie just called and said she was arrested and didn't have the money for bail. Ya'll band together and help me bring that queen home!"

Suddenly all of the people who were broke when I was on stage, dug into their purses with their wide knuckles and presented bills. I feel like spinning on these queens and scratching their cakey faces. Always hating on me but treating Charlie like he's some kind of rare queen. Just cause he knows how to do makeup and make wigs. What about me?

SHAY HUNTER

I'm here at least three times a week and Charlie is here no more than once a week if that. Where is the fucking loyalty?

A few of the queens look at me as they place their bills in the wig. I guess because I'm in here while he's in jail. I can feel their disapproving stares, including Sugar's who just shakes her head and walks away from me.

Trying to give a performance of a lifetime I say, "Oh my, God"— I cover my mouth— "I gotta get out of here and help my girl! She needs my help."

CHAPTER THREE

Charlie

It's cold in this jail cell, and the iron bench under me makes my back hurt. I'm doing all I can to stay warm. Like rubbing my arms, and pacing the floor but nothing seems to make me comfortable. At the end of the day all I want to do is go home, take a bath and think about what I'm going to do with my life, without having a job or money.

Earlier today when I called Dixie and the cell phone call dropped, I didn't know what I was going to do. Since I was only allowed one call, I knew I could possibly sit in jail for hours or days. But luckily the nice officer allowed me one more call and I decided to call club Wiggles, because I don't have a family. Outside of Dixie, the only associates I have are in that club.

I giggle as I remember when I called Wiggles earlier, and got a hold of Belize.

"They did what?" Belize yelled on the phone.

"They locked me up, and I need someone to come get me out."

"What they lock you up for, chile?"

I was embarrassed and unsure of what to tell her. I mean how do you say you got caught stealing from your job? Luckily Belize didn't keep me on the hook for too long.

"You know what, it doesn't even matter. If they got my bitch up in there she's coming out tonight. So excuse me while I go flip the wig, collect the coins and be there directly. Trust me, sweetie, Queen Be will have you out in no time."

A lot of people at the club don't like Belize. They say she's too big, too tall, loud and gets too many silicone injections in her face and ass. But she's always been real with me, and for that I appreciate her.

Although I was scared when my call with Dixie accidently dropped, because I didn't know what I was going to do, I was also slightly relieved. I didn't want to mess up Dixie's day. Dixie spent months trying to get on the line up for Wiggles, and I know she wanted it badly. Besides, she was due to make money. Even the worst girls got at least fifty bucks, with the headliners making a couple hundred. Although Dixie didn't need the job, because she's a G15 in the government, she's also always broke because she calls out regularly.

I was still thinking about Dixie when a man who caused my heart to skip was brought in. He was so handsome. His complexion was the color of coffee, with a little cream poured inside. He had to be about 6'5, which was the perfect height for me, a girl who loves her heels. His entire body was tatted up and my stomach fluttered. He was my kind of guy and my mind wandered on what our lives would be like, if he chose me. That is until I realize that men like him don't go for boys like me. I need to get out of jail, because I'm losing my mind now for real.

"I bet after a few hours in here, you'll calm down," the male officer says to him as he walks him into the cell in handcuffs. "You lucky we didn't hurt you for acting the way you did when we brought you in." The officer who was leading him into the cell was the same one who snatched my wig off.

"I bet you if I wasn't behind these bars, I'd reconstruct that face of yours," Mr. Tattoo says to the officer.

I could tell the officer was frightened because he said no more, and quickly locked the bars.

While Mr. Tattoo seemed to be completely oblivious to me being here, he was the only focus of my attention. While he's looking at the dirty floor, I

SHAY HUNTER

observe the bruises on his face, and wonder how he got them and who gave them to him. I want to ask if there's anything I can do, until I remember I am in jail too, and can't even pay my own bail. I'm useless.

"Mr. Monroe, you've made bail," the female officer says to me.

I quickly jump up because those were the sweetest words I heard all day. As I walk to the bars, I look at *Mr. I Gotta Have Him* one more time, but again he doesn't look my way.

When the door is open, slowly I follow the officer down the hall and to another counter. Within five minutes I'm processed and given my property back. But when I'm about to put my wig back on my head, I noticed it's damp. When I raise it to my nose to take a whiff, I can smell urine. I look behind the counter, at the officers who hated me from the moment I was brought in, and they are laughing hysterically.

"We wanted to give you a little something to remember us by," one of them says grabbing his crotch, "since you love dick so much."

I want to cry but demand myself not to. Instead I throw the five hundred dollar wig into the trash, and walk out of the doors. The moment the summer night breeze smacks my face, and I see Dixie's white Range Rover sparkling in the parking lot I smile.

Tranny 911

I run up to the truck and slide inside, placing my seat belt on. A few seconds later, I notice he's dressed in drag, and I thought that was kind of wrong since he knew I was locked up. His makeup doesn't cover the many freckles on his light skin, and he looks pretty bad. I know he didn't know my exact whereabouts, but couldn't he have called around? The moment I ask myself that question I realize how selfish I'm being.

Dixie allows me to stay in her house in Palmer Park Maryland rent-free. She cooks for me every night, and allows me to stash my money so that I can fix the damage Bernard did to my face, and save up for a sexual reassignment surgery. She's given me all she has too, and doesn't owe me anything else. I should be grateful.

"Thank you so much for coming to get me, Dixie." I push my seat back some. It feels good to be out. "I thought when the call dropped that—"

"You know this was an inconvenience right?" He says, pulling out of the parking lot. "You knew how much tonight meant to me, and still you had to go do dumb shit." He shakes his head. "I don't know, Charlie, but are you sure this shit wasn't done on purpose?"

"Of course not!"

"Then why would you do something so stupid on my big day?"

SHAY HUNTER

"I know how it looks, Dixie, and I'm sorry. I don't even know how they knew I was taking the money. I had always been so careful up to this point." I put my hands over my face. "I knew who was in the control station and watching the floor and everything." I speak into my hands. "I'm so confused."

"So you blaming everybody else, instead of your selfish ass?"

"No...I..."

"This is wrong, Charles. Wrong as shit."

"I know...I just..."

"And then you calling down Wiggles and asking for money. Putting people in our business. Making it look like I don't got my friend's back. You played me hard, Charlie. Real hard."

"I didn't think you got my message, Dixie. The call dropped like it always does with your phone. And I thought...I thought you didn't hear me, or knew where I was. I didn't want to stay in jail all night, but at no time was I trying to play you."

"But they flipped the wig, Charlie. You know they only flip the wig for emergencies. You weren't going to die if you had to sit in jail a few hours longer, especially it was your own fault to begin with." He shook his head. "I don't know, this time may be where I stop helping you. I'm starting to feel unappreciated again."

My eyes widen and my heartbeat quickens. You don't understand, if Dixie stops helping me I'm out on the streets. There is no one to call, or anybody else I can count on. He's it for me. And although the girls down Wiggles flipped the wig for me, they'd never let me stay in their homes, with their men, around their friends. I'm considered a 'Small Threat'.

We call girls who are considered cute, tiny and petite small threats because they have the potential to turn the heads of both straight and gay guys. It will never work, and I need his help.

I turn around and face him. "Dixie, I'm so sorry. I really am." I put my hand over my heart. "You are so right, I could've been a little more patient, and understood that you would've come looking for me. It was wrong to call down Wiggles and I will never do something like that again."

"Exactly," he yells. "You were wrong, way wrong. Because I take care of you but who's going to take care of me? Huh? All I wanted was the performance tonight and you ruined it. I couldn't even go on stage tonight."

"Oh my, god, I'm so sorry," I say. "And I can't take care of you but if I could I would. You know that."

"That's not good enough anymore, Charlie. I want more. I need more."

I look away and my voice shakes. "What do you want?"

SHAY HUNTER

Slowly Dixie pulls over to the side of the road. It's in a dark residential area, with a lot of trees and bushes. When he parks he rubs his hand along side my face. "You remember that day I saved you? After Bernard beat you the way that he did?"

"Yes," I nod.

"You remember how I convinced my mother into letting you stay with me, even though she didn't want you too?"

"Yes, Dixie. I remember all of the wonderful things you did for me. And I'm forever grateful."

"I've always been good to you, haven't I?"

I look into his eyes and observe his facial expression. Although he was wearing a wig and a dress, he doesn't look feminine. He looks out of place. He looks spooky.

"You have always taken care of me, Dixie. And all I can say is one day, when I can, I'm going to take care of you too."

"I know you are, beautiful, and that day is going to start now." He raises his dress and tears pour out of my eyes.

"Dixie, no," I shake my head. "You promised that you'd never make me do it again. Remember? You said that after the last time, you wouldn't blackmail me into doing this, just to have a place to live. You promised, Dixie!"

"So I blackmail you now?" He frowns. "Because I'm asking that you take care of me?"

"No," I wipe my tears. "Those were your words, not mine. You were the one who said you'd never *blackmail* me again."

"And if they are mine, and if I did say blackmail, I can take my words back. Now, get over here and suck my dick, and make it extra wet too. I got a lot on my mind."

"Please, Dixie!"

"You want me to put you out of my car and house? You think you can find a better living arrangement, than the one you have with me?"

"No."

"Then do it now."

I can tell in his eyes that he wants what he wants. No amount of tears or words will change a thing. So I do exactly what he says. Besides, what other choice do I have?

CHAPTER FOUR

Dixie

I'm pounding this wrinkled bitch out from the back in her house. Although Griselda is eighty years old and counting, the bitch got a sex drive that would put a teenager to shame. And the pussy ain't bad either. She was always wanting me to fuck her longer and harder and it felt like I could never satisfy her fully.

"Hit it from the back, Dixon," she coaches. "Harder." I pound her harder. "Harder got damn it! Give it to me like you do them young dumb bitches! I can take it! Don't let the wrinkles fool you."

This time I pump her so hard, her gray hair slams into the wooden headboard. Before I know it she's spilling her milk all over my dick. And even though she can't get pregnant, I splash my nut into the condom.

When we're done she rolls over on the bed and smiles at me. Her white wrinkle breasts fall to the sides of her body. "What did I do to deserve you?" she asks me.

I wipe my dick using the tissues on the side of the table. "You take care of me. So you've proven that you deserve me."

"And you take care of me too," she reminds me. "That dick just gets better and better with time, young man." She licks her lips. "How do you do it?"

That's the only thing about Griselda I like. When it comes to the money, the old bitch spares no expenses on me. Whatever I want, she buys. I don't care what it is. Before my mother disappeared, she was her best friend. I remember when Griselda use to come over, with fresh baked cakes and pies for the church, and she couldn't keep her eyes off of me. When my mother wasn't looking, she would always slide me over a fresh twenty-dollar bill if I flipped her clit while she sat on the toilet in our bathroom pissing. She was a freak of the worst kind, and I cashed out on her many times.

"That's because you're my man," she says. "And I love taking care of what's mine."

What a stupid old bitch. "Sure I'm yours, all yours. But look, my truck has been giving me trouble again. You gonna break me off something?"

SHAY HUNTER

The smile on her face fades away. "It's been kind of hard around here, Dixon. I haven't gotten my check and—"

"You not keeping your end of the deal," I say to her seriously, "G, you said as long as I took care of you sexually, you would take care of me. I came over here and just fucked your brains out. So what's changed now? If you can't handle the relationship let me know."

"I can, I can," she repeats sitting up in the bed. "It's just that, I've been having to borrow money from family lately. They're talking about placing me in a home, because they don't know where the money is going."

"You know what, I'm going home," I grab my gray sweat pants off of the floor. "I see you're a fucking liar and I can't play that game with you any more. You know I need your help and you promised to always help me."

"Don't leave, please," she says. I look at her and wait for something I want to hear. "Get my purse over there on the dresser, I have a couple hundred dollars in there."

"That's my girl," I say as I grab the brown leather purse. She shuffles through it and hands me my money. "But look, let me go clean up right quick, G. And if you want to go another round, I'm with that too. You know I like to take care of my baby."

She spreads her wrinkled legs and fingers her pink pussy. "And you know I'm gonna be ready too. Hurry up out. I'm going to take a shower in the other room, so that I can be fresh with you."

I shake my head and walk to the bathroom. It had been a week since I bailed Charles out from jail, and every day since then the tension has been thick in our house. If he wasn't moping around about not having a job, he was crying about possibly going to jail. And when I would try to console him, he would jump like I was going to do something to him.

If he's still uneasy just because I made him suck my dick, he can kill himself. As far as I'm concerned, considering everything I do for him, he should be asking to break me off the moment I hit the doors. Instead he wants to whine and cry, talking about friends don't do friends like that. Fuck him.

After I wash my face, and look at myself in the mirror I realize I'm confused. Part of me wants to be as beautiful as Charlie, and then the other part of me, likes the rough side I was born with. Like right now I'm staring at my natural short red hair, and my red face which has a five o'clock shadow.

Whenever I come over here I butch it out. I wear sneakers, jeans and baggy clothes to fit the mood. Griselda likes to see me like this, because it turns her on and she knows nothing about my gay lifestyle.

SHAY HUNTER

One time I made a mistake and left my black nail polish on, after going to Wiggles the night before and it took me two hours to explain why I had it on. When she pointed it out I pretended to be a Dennis Rodman fan, and since it was his birthday, she let it go.

After getting myself cleaned up, and forming a good lie on why I had to bounce early, I open the bathroom door. The moment I walk into her room, I knew something was off. She said she was going to take a shower but why wasn't she back.

"G, where you at?" I ask placing my wallet into my pants. "Griselda, where are you? I have to go!"

"My mother is in the kitchen right now," someone says entering the room.

When I turn around, I'm looking at Berry, her only son.

"Oh, what's up man, I haven't seen you in awhile."

This is bad. There is absolutely no reason for me to be in this house.

"Cut the shit, Dixon. Have you been coming over here and taking my mother's money? Huh?" he steps closer to me and I step back. "Lately her bank account has been dry and I'm not understanding why. Can you explain this to me?"

"Listen, it's not the way you think it is. I just…"

"Been using her." He frowns. "What the fuck is up with that? My mother is practically your mother. We grew up together and everything, man. She's old as shit! Eighty years old! What kind of sick shit is this?"

"I know how it looks but…"

"She told me the truth, Dixon," he replies waving his hand. "So before you lie to me, understand that she told me everything already."

When I look down at his side, I see the shape of a gun handle under his shirt. "So what you saying? You came here to kill me? Over some fucking money?"

"I'm saying you need to give me a reason why—"

I hit Berry in the face so hard, I know he doesn't see it coming. When he's down on the floor, he tries to go for his gun but I'm already on top of him. I steal him in the face again, and then wrestle the gun away from him. The moment I have it in my hand, I feel powerful.

"Don't shoot me, man, please," he begs from the floor, as I stand over top of him.

"Give me a reason why I shouldn't."

"Because—"

I pull the trigger and blow his brains back without even waiting. When his mother rushes into the room, and sees what I've done, I shoot her too.

SHAY HUNTER

Her body slumps over his and I look down at them both.

I feel no remorse.

CHAPTER FIVE

Charlie

I'm watching the queens, whose makeup and hair I did earlier perform on the stage as Destiny's Child. They are so beautiful and look so much like women, I almost forget they are men. Their body's move and sway all over the stage and they look like ballerinas. Amazing!

"You outdid yourself this time," Dixie says to me as we both watch their routine. "How the hell you cover Ms. Ralph's five o'clock shadow? I can't even see her hair!"

"It wasn't easy because you know he doesn't like to cut it, so that he can appear butch when he goes to work. But I made it do what it do, chile." I continue to look up at him.

SHAY HUNTER

When they finish performing, I notice Kenny Sugar is walking in my direction. "I been wondering where Sugar has been." I say to myself.

"Girl, well don't wonder too long. Let's get out of here," Dixie says grabbing my hand. "I don't trust that queen. I hear he be killing mothafuckas."

Before he can pull me out of the club, Sugar is upon me. In the gay community Sugar is a legend so I feel star struck in his presence. He's the one the girls go to when they want injections and he's the best in the business. Any queen you see in Wiggles with a knotty butt, face or hips is not Sugar's work. He's an artist.

Before my stash was compromised due to having to pay Dixie back for the bail, I planned to use some of my money on him. I wanted butt injections, because mine wasn't big enough, and the surgeries the doctors perform don't work. I also want hips because I barely had any, and I planned to purchase my breasts too. But my money is gone and now all I can do is hope and pray that I'll get my nest egg back up so that I can afford Sugar.

When Sugar approaches me wearing a long black maxi dress and a red suit jacket I'm thrown off. She looks bad. She looks tired. Although she works miracles for her clients, she doesn't take care of herself well at all. Maybe she's too busy.

At 5'5, she's sloppy and I can still see the stubble on her face, compliments of her manhood. Her mascara is always runny and her light skin seems smacked with too much foundation and blush. With all of that, he's still a star in my eyes. Outside of his great work with injections, there's one other thing I heard about Sugar that made me look up to him. I heard he's like a Dutch uncle, the kind of person who will always tell you the truth. In my opinion that's refreshing.

"Ms. Charlie, you sure are a hard girl to get in contact with," he says to me, with a big smile. He hugs me tightly and lets me go. "And just as beautiful as the day is long. Seems like you get more gorge with time. How do you do it?"

I shrug. "I don't know," I grin. "But did you say that you've been trying to get in contact with me?" I point to myself. What could the legend want with me?

"Yes, your friend over here didn't tell you?" he asks, giving Dixie and evil look. "Because I've run him down at least ten times that I can think of."

I shake my head slowly and look back at him. "Maybe he forgot."

"Don't you go making excuses for him," Sugar says sternly. "Like I said I've come to him at least ten times asking about you, and each time he tells me he'll give you my message. Tell him, Dixie. Am I lying or not?"

Dixie rolls his eyes. "I got more important stuff to do than to be running behind Charlie, giving him your messages. I don't work for the phone company. I'm employed with the government. If you want to tell him something, tell him your damn self."

Sugar shakes his head. "Anyway, none of that matters. Since you are here I was wondering if I could use your services."

"My services?" I smile. "What do you mean?"

"It's no secret that you are a beast with that paintbrush. I've seen you do the makeup on some of the queens around here so good, I wish they could sleep in it instead of taking it off. You're a genius, Ms. Charlie. And don't get me started on that hot comb! I've never seen anybody create wigs or style hair better than you. You are a ball of talent over-flowing, girl!"

I try not to blush but I can't help it. "Thank you, Sugar. Coming from you that means a lot."

"Well I'm serious, because Ms. Sugar doesn't say anything he doesn't mean. I mean look at you now." He takes my hand and spins me around. "That face is beat, that Gilda (wig) is on point and you have a body that won't quit. You could fool the straightest of men, Ms. Charlie."

Now I feel like he's lying. I hate everything about my body and couldn't wait to do something about it. "If you say so."

"I'm serious. I have women who would kill for hips like yours. And if you've seen Ms. Sugar's bank account, you would know that I'm serious." He pauses. "Anyway, enough of the truth, since I see you can't handle it. How about I get to my reason for approaching you. As you know I do pumping parties, and just recently I've broadened my scope of practice. A lot of the queens who come see me are in need of an entire makeover before going to the balls. That's where you come in. I have a few Total Makeover parties scheduled in the near future, and I could use your help. In turn I'll teach you everything you want to know about the business."

"When you say business…are you…talking about…"

"I'm talking about that for the first time in history, Ms. Sugar is willing to teach someone else what she does. I'm going to show you how to inject."

I almost choke on my tongue. Not only would learning his business put me in a position to earn money, but it would also show me how to do some things on myself if need be.

Before I could say yes Dixie says, "Charlie not getting involved in all that shit you selling. She values her freedom and injecting folks without a license won't do shit but get her locked up."

"I'm sorry, honey, but did I give the microphone to you?" Sugar asks him.

"You don't have to, I took it."

Sugar shakes his head, rolls his eyes and then focuses back on me. "Charlie, I'm going to be real with you, you have a leech on your hands." She looks at Dixie and then back at me. "Now the sooner you realize it, the better off you'll be. But I'm going to leave you to your own problems, as far as he's concerned anyway."

"This old hag swears she knows me," Dixie says.

"I most certainly do," Sugar replies. And then he digs into his pocket and pulls something out. "Now here is my card."

It was plain, white and had his number written on it in pen. It wasn't what I would expect him to be using.

"Thank you," I say staring at it. While feeling it's texture.

"If you want to make money, call me there. I must warn you though. That my number changes every thirty days, for safety reasons. In my line of business I appreciate changing numbers. So I hope to hear from you soon." He looks at Dixie once more, and then walks away.

"I can't stand that mothafucka," Dixie says.

I was so excited that I forgot he was even there. I feel like I just hit the lottery.

"Look at him, looking like an old faggy," Dixie shakes his head.

As he talks shit about him, I examine his gear. Although he's dressed in drag too, you can still see his masculine ways. The red dress and old curly wig he's wearing makes him look sixty-five instead of twenty-three like we both are.

"You gotta stay away from him, Charlie. Trust me."

"Why?"

"Like I said before he came over here, I heard he be killing faggies on purpose with them silicone injections and shit. That fat mothafucka is foul!"

I frown. "I never heard anything like that."

"Well you're hearing it from me now. Like I said, if I were you, I'd stay away from him. You've been warned."

<hr/>

I'm standing outside of the club smoking a cigarette when a cutie pulls up in front of me on the curb. He's driving a red BMW. "Hi you doing, beautiful," he says to me. "I haven't seen anything as gorgeous as you in a long time."

He's wearing a Brooklyn Nets basketball cap and it's hiding the top part of his eyes.

I smile. "I'm good." I drop the cigarette on the ground and stamp it out with my black pumps.

"I wish I could be good with you," he says. "You think you can make that happen with me?"

I laugh. "You gotta come better than that, sweetheart. That line you gave might work on the little girls but I need something more official."

SHAY HUNTER

He chuckles. "You right, you right, ma." He says nodding his head. "You got me. But look, I was wondering if we could spend a little time together, maybe hang out, and grab something to eat. That's if you ain't doing nothing right now."

I want to say yes, because it's been a long time since I've been in the company of a man, but I remember what Sugar says. As I look down at myself I realize how easy it is for me to pass off as a woman. Does he think I'm one now?

"You know I'm a—"

"I know that already." He frowns. "You coming or not?"

I don't know how I always end up in these situations. But an hour later, I'm in the back of Greg's BMW, getting banged out from behind. As he pushes into my body, I imagine that he's mine. I imagine that he loves me and that I love him back. If I do it good enough maybe he'll stay around, or at the very least, he'll want to do it again. It doesn't matter that I just met him, because for the moment anyway, it's real.

After he moans loudly, and cums inside of me, just like the other times with strangers, he switches off and his mood changes.

"Your stomach flat, ma," he says pulling up his pants and easing into the driver's seat, "you never had any kids?"

Chill bumps rise over my body, as I look at him strangely. "How could I have kids?"

"What you mean how could you have kids?" he turns his car on. "You're a beautiful woman? Did you at least try?"

"I told you back there, that I'm a—"

"If you tell me you're a man I'm going to go off on you." His expression is sinister and my body trembles.

He doesn't want to hear the truth. Just like how I allowed my imagination to roam free when we were having sex, he wants his imagination to roam now. He wants to pretend that he doesn't know that I'm a man.

"I know that's not what you're about to say right? I know you not crazy enough to fake like you're a man, with a nigga like me." When I look down in his lap I see a gun. "As a matta of fact get the fuck out of my car." When I don't move fast enough he yells, "Bounce!"

As he pulls off, almost running over my toes in the process, I wonder if this will continue to be my life.

SHAY HUNTER

CHAPTER SIX

Charlie

"I'm so glad you called, Charlie," Sugar says to me, as we sit in an upscale restaurant in Washington, DC. "The funny thing is, I was just about to change the number. I'm glad I didn't, because I would've missed your call."

When a waiter walks up to us, he takes Sugar's order and then focuses on me. I didn't have a job and I only had 50 bucks to my name. So I had to be very careful about what I bought or spent. Everything on the menu was so expensive; and the only thing I could afford was a side salad.

"I'll take a side salad, and a water with lemon please." I hand him the menu.

"Charlie, are you serious? We come to this beautiful restaurant and all you want is a salad?"

I lean in so that the waiter can't hear my voice. "I'm going to be real with you, I can't afford to eat in here."

He focuses on the waiter and says, "You can bring what she wanted but she'll also have the biggest steak on your menu, and bring out your finest bottle of wine too."

"How would you like that steak cooked, ma'am?" he asks me.

I'm so stunned. In all of my life nobody has ever spent this kind of money on me before. "Well done please."

"No problem," the waiter says. "I'll be right back with your drinks." He walks away.

"Charlie, I don't know what kind of queens you rolled with before, but when a real bitch invites you out to dinner she takes the tab. Remember that shit and it will help you decide properly before accepting an invitation."

Feeling slightly stupid I say, "I appreciate it."

"Say no more," he smiles. "We'll talk about business in a moment, but first what is your real relationship with Dixon?"

"What do you mean? He's my best friend."

"He seems very overprotective for someone who supposed to be only a friend." He drinks his water.

SHAY HUNTER

"We are friends, but a little more than that," I say placing the curls behind my ear.

The waiter brings the wine back over and pours a little in Sugar's glass. Sugar shakes the glass, sniffs it, sips it and nods, which causes the waiter to proceed to pour both of us glasses and I'm relieved. I need something to calm my nerves down.

When he leaves Sugar says, "Please tell me you're not sleeping with that toad! You're much too beautiful for him."

I think about all the times he blackmailed me into giving him blowjobs. I think about how he looks at me sometimes when he catches me walking out of the room naked.

Although I'm not interested in Dixon sexually, in the back of my mind I know he looks at me that way. But, I can't tell anyone, partially because I'm loyal and also because the topic is so weird to think about that I get embarrassed.

"No, it's nothing like that. It's kind of hard to explain. Let's just say that he's been there for me when nobody else has."

"Then let me be frank with you. He's going to bring you down before it's all said and done. I've come across a lot of queens in my lifetime, and he's by far the worst. Just be careful."

"I'm sure I'll be fine, but I appreciate your concern."

"Now let's get on to the subject at hand. As you know they call me the Pumping Queen. But to tell you the truth I'm tired of the business. And I'm looking for someone who already has a skill set so that I can pass on what I've learned."

"And you want that person to be me?" I place my hand over my chest.

That's why we're here, darling."

"But I don't know what to do." I sip my wine, I think out of nervousness more than anything else. "I never even considered doing injections before. What if I hurt someone?"

"You'll hurt many people. The procedure is not kind and it is very painful."

"I don't know, Sugar," I say softly.

"You need the money?"

"Of course I do!"

"Then that's all we need to focus on, I'll teach you the rest. But, let me clear something up, I don't want Dixie anywhere near my business. You may trust her but I don't. Do we have a clear understanding as far as she's concerned?"

"We do," I respond.

I'm just about to dig into my wine when my cell phone rings. When I look at the cell phone I see Dixon's telephone number. I don't know what makes me answer but I do.

"Excuse me for a minute," I say placing one finger up. "Hello."

SHAY HUNTER

"Charlie, where are you?" He asks me. His voice sounds frantic.

But because I don't want him to know that I'm with Sugar, I change the subject. "Are you okay? You don't sound too good."

"That's why I'm calling you. I need you to come home, I'm having more chest pains."

Ever since I could remember Dixon always had chest pains. He was born with a heart murmur, and he was in and out of the hospital, and my greatest fear was that one-day one of his episodes would lead to death. Although it hasn't happened yet, it stays in the back of my mind.

"Oh my God! I'm on my way home now!"

When I end the call Sugar says, "Is everything okay?"

"I'm so sorry, Sugar, but I have to leave." I sip all of my wine, stand up and grab my purse. "Something is wrong with Dixie.

I don't like the look that Sugar is giving me. It's like he doesn't believe that Dixie is in real pain. Although Sugar is cool, Dixie has supported me throughout my ordeal with my father and I owe him my loyalty. I would never turn my back on him for anything or anyone.

"You do what you have to do, sweetheart," he says. "Reach out to me when you can, and when you're ready to do business."

I'm exhausted when I finally make it home. I park my beat down green Nissan Altima and ease out the car. Before I get inside I can hear Dixie's voice. He's talking on the phone and he doesn't sound the slightest bit sick to me.

"Bitch, I'm going to kill it when we go to Wiggles tomorrow night! There ain't a chick in the world that will have anything on me this time."

Something comes over me at that moment, although I know that it is wrong to feel this way. Although it's possible to be sick and still hold a conversation, he seems a little too chipper for me.

So I turn around and walk back towards my car. Once inside, I call Sugar. "Sugar, I'm on my way back. Turns out it was a false alarm."

"I told you that bitch was faking."

SHAY HUNTER

CHAPTER SEVEN

Dixie

This bitch is trying it with me today, but it's cool. Yesterday I told Charlie I needed his help, because I was having chest pains and I wanted him to take me to the hospital. But instead of him coming home to check on me, he didn't show up until three in the morning. And then when he does get in, instead of asking me if I'm okay, he ignores me and goes straight to his bedroom, talking about he's tired and to leave him alone. What kind of shit is that?

I'm in the living room with my legs crossed steaming mad. I'm looking at the two pink small luggage suitcases by the door, which holds his make up and irons for when he does hair and styles his wigs. I bought all of that shit because with the job he had at FloorMart, he wasn't able to afford a thing. I virtually made him, and this is how he treats me? Little does he know, I got some shit in motion for that ass.

To hear Fergie tell it I should leave him alone, because of everything that has happened to him, because he didn't have a father or mother in his life. But I did all I was required to and more. If it wasn't for me the nigga would be out on the streets. Since he lost his job, and got arrested, I'm the one who takes care of him. I buy the food. I pay the mortgage and I cook. Literally all Charlie has to do is makeup my face when I drag it out, or my hair when I want a little length. That's it.

Since he wants to have an attitude, for only god knows what, I decide to play her little game. The good thing about Charlie is this, unlike some people he'll spend an hour in the shower, which pisses me off if I have things to do. It's so bad that I have to get in the tub before he does, because if I don't the water will run cold leaving me with none. Now I'm going to use this huge fault against him in a major way.

The first thing I do is place the dining room chair under the door so that he can't get out. When that is done, I grab a water jug and then roll his suitcases outside and throw them in the trunk of my car. Then I drive to a dumpster behind the back of Wendy's, and throw them inside. All of his makeup, his hair irons and everything else is now gone. Since I bought that shit, I also have the right to discard it too.

When I make it back home, before going inside, I pour the water in the gas tank of his car. *Yeah, bitch. Wherever you go, it won't be too far tonight. That you can be sure of.*

When I make it back inside of my house, I shake my head when I realize he's still in the shower. I mean how fresh do a bitch gotta be? Since he's still unavailable, I kindly mess up the living room. I knock down flower vases, which spills water all over my hardwood floors. Then I rush into his bedroom and open up the dressers, and throw out things, before doing the same to my room. When I'm done doing my thing, it looks like something terrible has ripped through the house.

With my scene set, I remove the chair from the doorknob just as the water is turned off in the shower. Finally I lay on the floor in the hallway and the moment Charlie comes out I yell, "Help, help! We've been robbed!"

"You act like you don't believe me," I say to her, while I'm sitting on the sofa. "Somebody took us for everything we got."

Tranny 911

"But I don't understand," she says pacing the floor. "When did this supposedly happen?" Charlie has a towel wrapped around his lower body and I can't get over how feminine he looks. "I didn't hear anything."

"You were in the shower, and if you ask me, I think Sugar had something to do with this shit. I keep trying to tell you to stop bringing new people in the picture but you don't listen."

"Sugar," she says wiping tears from her eyes. "Why would she do something like this? I've hung out with her several times and she's never gave me the impression that she'd ever do anything like this."

"Because she's sneaky, Charlie! That's what I been trying to tell you about that bitch. You so busy running around town with him that you don't even care what kind of person you are hanging with. You gotta mind the company you keep."

"But Sugar has money. He don't need ours."

"You a fool if you really believe that. You see how broke down that queen dresses."

"Even if that was the case, why would she want to steal my makeup kit? And my curling irons?" she rubbed her temples. "It doesn't make any sense to me, Dixie."

"I'm starting to feel differently about you, Charlie."

"What is that supposed to mean?"

"Before you started hanging with Sugar, we trusted each other. And now that you are supposedly working for him, and making money that you probably will never see, suddenly you forget your past."

"Dixie, you should know something, I came home last night early."

"And?" I shrug.

"I heard you on the phone talking to Fergie. You were loud and ridiculous and you didn't sound like anything was wrong with you. If anything, you were the one who sounded weird." She places her clothes on that are folded on the chair.

This the type of shit I be talking about right here. Had he not been hanging with Sugar, he would've never tried a snake like move like that, by listening to the door instead of coming in. Yes it is true that my chest wasn't hurting, but he didn't know that shit. The only reason I lied, was to get him away from Sugar because I don't trust him. If anything I'm saving his life and this is the thanks I get.

"Loud and ridiculous? That's what you think of me?" I stand up. "Charlie, if you must know, I took something for the pain. So when you came home only to be sneaky, you caught me at a better time. You know I been dealing with chest pains all of my life. I was born with a heart murmur."

"I know," he says in a low voice. "You won't let me forget." He sat on the recliner and slid into his shoes.

"You know but you do me like this?" Suddenly I start to cry. "Charlie, you are so disloyal right now! We were robbed and look at what they did to the house." I look behind me so that Charlie can see the damage to the flower vases. "And then I had chest pains last night, and the way you acting, I'll have chest pains tonight too."

"Well maybe you should sit down," he replies.

"Sit down? SIT DOWN!"

Charlie stands up and suddenly he looks bad for talking to me this way. "I'm sorry, Dixie, please forgive me. But you have to understand, I just lost all of my equipment. I'm fucked up right now."

"Fuck forgiveness! We are supposed to have a bond. And you breaking it right now."

I know some may think I'm doing stunts and shows, but Charlie deserves all of this shit. Had he not chose a traitor over me, I wouldn't have to make him feel this pain. But he did, and now he must see what it feels like to be betrayed.

"Dixie, I really am sorry." He says softly. "I just…I just don't know what's going on right now. When I lost my job I got all turned around in the head and I haven't been myself lately. All I want to do is get a little money so that I can get a lawyer."

"I told you I would buy your lawyer," I say wiping my tears.

SHAY HUNTER

"But I don't want you to do that. I know you do everything for me as is, and for once I wanted your only focus to be you."

"You know what," I walk to the door. "I want you to get out of my house." I hold the door open.

Her eyes widen. "But I don't have anywhere to go."

"Charlie, get the fuck out of my house, because that's not my problem. And while you're out there, tell me if Sugar will let you stay with her, since she stays up in my business anyway."

CHAPTER EIGHT

Charlie

As I walk to my car, I realize I need something to change in my life right away. I can't keep going through this. The relationship between Dixie and me has gotten out of control, and I hate living like this. Everyday I live in fear that I'm going to do or say something that will cause him to throw me out. Even though I've been here for years, I never felt like I had a place of my own, and I'm getting the feeling that he likes it like that.

I get in my car and drive on the way to Sugar's house. I don't have my cell phone so I can't even call him and tell him I'm on my way. What the fuck am I going to do?

When my car starts sputtering, my heart drops. What the fuck is going on now? I pull over to the side of the road, and cut the car off. After a minute I turn it back on, but don't allow the engine to wake up. Instead I eye the lit dashboard hoping it will tell me what's going on. When it doesn't, I turn the key again but the engine doesn't start.

"Why is this happening to me?" I say to myself. "Please tell me why terrible things always seem to follow me?"

I'm hitting my steering wheel, when all of a sudden a dude pulls up in a white work truck. On the side of the truck is a green sign that reads *Platinum Detailing Shop*. He parks next to me, rolls his window down and says, "Are you okay? You look like you having a bad day."

"No, my car wont' start," I can feel my face flush. He's so handsome.

"Want me to check it out? I mean I have a few minutes on my hand, and I don't mind."

I shrug and my lips curl into a semi smile. "If you want to, I would really appreciate your help."

When he gets out of the truck, I can't believe how tall he is. The light green shirt, and the dark green pants he's wearing hang off of his body smoothly. He's definitely in shape. And there's something about a blue-collar man that just does it for me. Then I remember, since I'm in drag, he probably thinks I'm a woman, and my hopes are suddenly stopped. He'll never be attracted to me if he learns who I really am.

He walks in front of the car and says, "Pop the hood, beautiful."

I do, and he grabs a white towel from his back pocket. Then he takes out a long stick from under my hood and wipes it off on the towel. When he's done with that, he puts it back and walks to my gas tank. He looks like he's really knows what he's doing. I'm very lucky.

He does all of that and then walks up to my window and says, "I have no idea what's wrong with your car."

I break out into a heavy laughter.

"Damn, I wasn't that funny was I?"

"It isn't you," I say. "It's just been a crazy day. But thanks for trying to help me."

He closes my hood and walk toward the driver's side window. "Look, do you need me to drop you off anywhere? Ain't no need in staying out here by yourself at night, and I'm finished with my work for the day."

My eyebrows rise. "If you can that would be sooooo good."

He opens my car door, and offers me his hand. I step out and catch him looking at my ass, but when I look at him he tries to turn away. "And don't worry about your car. You can give me your address, and

SHAY HUNTER

I'll have someone tow it from here to my auto body shop."

"But what about later tonight?"

"Well that's where I come in. Since you don't have your car, and I feel partially responsible for you, I'm going to have to wait on you to take you home. And before you say no, I don't accept no for an answer."

"But I can't let you do all of that."

"It ain't about letting me do anything. It's about me doing something that I want, for a beautiful woman. Can you understand that?"

I blush, and bite my bottom lip. "If you say so."

"I do say so." He winks. "So give me the address. I'll take you to wherever you want to go."

I am in a hotel suite in Bethesda Maryland, and there are so many gay men inside waiting to receive work from Sugar, that there isn't a place for me to sit down anywhere.

I'm walking with her when Sugar grabs a sign in sheet from his assistant Sunshine and says to me, "I don't know why you didn't call me earlier, Charlie. You didn't have to be on the side of the road, I would've come to get you."

"I know but you're so busy," I say looking around. "I swear I don't see how you do this. This place is jammed pack."

"Girl, it ain't about nothing, I'm use to it now. My only problem is that I don't get to take care of myself, because my life evolves around this work. But that's what I got you here for right?" he hands Sunshine the sign in sheet.

"I just hope I don't let you down."

"You won't, and don't even worry about your makeup. One of my clients gets me everything new from Mac that drops. It's all in the back of my car, and you can grab it after you sit in on this procedure I'm about to do. Follow me."

I follow Sugar into another room within the suite and a queen is laying face down on the bed, with her butt in the air. Sugar looks at her assistant and says, "You applied the numbing cream already right?"

"Yep, she's all ready to go."

We walk over to the bed and I try not to look at the queen in her condition. It's bad enough she doesn't know me, but it's another thing to have me staring at her with her dick peeking out between her legs.

When I look at the dresser by the bed, I see a large red bowl of cotton balls and about twenty tubes of Krazy glue. Next to all of that, sits a jug of something white and creamy along with a syringe and a needle.

"How you doing, Natalie," Sugar says to him. "Everything okay? Are you comfortable?"

"I'm fine," she says softly, "I just want to get this over that's all."

"This is my other assistant Lindsay," he says to Natalie. "She'll be overseeing the procedure today."

"Okay," she says softly. "Whatever you need to do."

Without another word, Sugar pours the creamy white substance into the coffee cup, and then grabs the syringe pump and sucks up the creamy potion. I guess it's the silicone.

When she's done she twists on the needle and says, "I do thirty injections in each cheek, Lindsay. Ten on the top, ten in the middle and ten on the bottom." I nod and observe her closely.

Sugar places the first needle in Natalie's lower butt and the she jumps, and screams.

"I know it's painful, but you can't do that again. And while I'm at it you need to know that it will only get worse from here."

"I'm sorry, I didn't know it would feel so bad. It feels like lightning is striking me. I thought the numbing cream would make it feel better."

"That's the nature of the beast darling," Sugar replies. "And every girl out there, who is waiting for my services, knows it. Do you want me to continue or would you like to give up and go home?"

"I'll deal with it," she replies.

"Good, now be *very* still, before I think you can't handle it and be forced to give you half of your money back along with half of an ass cheek."

Although tears roll down Natalie's face, she remains silent and still for the rest of the procedure. As Sugar continues her job until all of the silicon has been pushed into her body. When Natalie is done, Sugar places crazy glue on the cotton balls and sticks them onto the injection sites.

My jaw drops. I never knew Krazy Glue could be used for surgeries too. When Sugar is done, the girl has an ass full of cotton balls. But the moment she stands up, I can already see the difference in her body. Her butt is rounder and her shape is filled out. It's amazing, and I see why people use his services.

"Before you leave I have to check your cotton." Sugar turns the girl around and squeezes each ball, when she finds one that is damp with silicone; she grabs the Krazy Glue and places it on the injection site, before adding another cotton ball. "You're good to go now, girlie."

"Thank you," Natalie says weakly, pulling her sweatpants up.

"Before you leave I have to go over a few things, since this is your first time. Number one, you are not to pull the cotton balls off. In order to remove them, you must soak in a tub of warm water tomorrow, and rub them off gently. If you do it too roughly they will leak and you'll lose silicone."

"Okay," she responds.

"Also, you need to massage your ass well for the next two weeks. Now it will feel uncomfortable but that's the nature of the beast too. It's important to get all of the silicone distributed evenly otherwise your ass will get rocky, and I don't want anybody thinking that's my work. You got it?'

She nods.

"Good, now you may go."

When the girl leaves out of the room I say, "You do this how often?"

"At least ten times a day, about five days a week." She pauses. "This is why I desperately need your help. So do you think you could do something like that?"

"If I really tried."

"Well that's what I'm hoping for. But I want to tell you something else too, you should never, ever, do procedures on the breasts. They are too close to the heart and can cause them immediate death. Never!" When someone knocks at the door Sugar is immediately agitated. "Who the fuck is that, when you know I don't like to be disturbed?"

"It's me, Sunshine. It's an emergency."

Sunshine opens the door and looks at me. "Your roommate Dixie just called here. I don't know how she got the number to the hotel, but she says to let you know she's in the hospital, and that you have to come now. She thinks she's dying."

SHAY HUNTER

CHAPTER NINE

Dixie

I'm lying in a hospital bed with an IV in my arm. I've been here for two hours, and already I'm ready to go home. Especially when the doctor offered to have me talk to a psychiatrist, like something's wrong with my head. I hate to take things this far, by faking chest pains and all, but Charlie needs to see what can happen if I were gone or if I were to die.

When I see Charlie being led into the back where I am, I get into character. But when I see who she's with I get annoyed all over again. Why couldn't she come by herself?

"You can only stay for thirty minutes," the doctor says to them. "After that I'm going to have to ask you both to leave."

"Dixie, are you okay," Charlie says grabbing my hand softly. "I was so fucking worried about you."

"If I were okay, would I really be here?" I ask rubbing my chest. "You know I have a heart murmur." I look at her man. "And who's that?"

"This is my new friend Nate. When I left the house, my car acted up on me and he gave me a ride to where I was going, and Sugar's house too."

My chest squeezes with anger. "You just gotta be around that bitch don't you? After everything, you just have to be around her. I mean, what is it about her that does it for you? I gotta know."

"Dixie, I know you don't believe me, but for real it's all about the money. I need it, and right now she can give it to me. I don't mean to hurt you, sweetheart, I really don't."

"So what are you, some sort of prostitute or something?"

I sit back in the bed. "No, it's nothing like that. It's just that, well, what else can I do? She has work for me and I have to take it."

"Whatever," I say.

"Let's not fight, Dixie. Right now the only thing on my mind is you." He rubs my hair. "Is there

SHAY HUNTER

anything I can do for you? I mean, are you in pain or anything?"

"You've done enough for me already, Charlie, I'm good..."

She sighs. "Dixie, I know we got into it today, and I know you told me to get out of the house. But, this kind of thing is the reason I can't move out right now. I mean, what if you couldn't call the police? Or reach the phone? In your condition you need me around, you know that."

"Charlie, if I had to count on you, I guess I would've died."

When her friend rolls his eyes I say, "Can you leave us alone?" He walks away without saying anything. "Charlie, you really hurt my feelings tonight, and you'll never know how much."

"I know, I really do, and I wish there was something I could do to take it back."

"There is, all you gotta do is stop hanging around Sugar. That alone will show me where your loyalty lies."

"How about this...Sugar is showing me how to do her procedures. For whatever reason, she's trusting me with everything she knows, and that's major, Dixie."

"Including her client list?"

"I'm not sure, but it looks like she won't hold back anything. Anyway the moment I learn all there is to learn about injections, I'll kindly tell her that I can't work with her anymore. And then I'll start my own business."

"How do I know you'll do it, Charlie?"

"Because my friendship is more important with you, Dixie. And I know I don't say it enough, but I appreciate everything you ever did for me. *Everything*. I just want a chance to take care of you like you did for me. When that money starts rolling in, I'm going to pay up your rent for three months in advance and you can stash your money in your purse, honey."

"Why you going to do all of that?"

"Because I love you that's why. And I don't want you in here hurt, or having a heart attack because of me. Does the doctor even know what's going on yet?"

"No. They're running tests."

She sighs. "Well I don't care what that bitch says, I'm going to be in here until they throw me out. If they gotta lock me up oh well, I need to know what's going on."

As she sits next to me on my bed I think about our friendship. Sometimes I do too much but it's only to make sure she doesn't go too far. I won't have my heart broken again, for nobody.

SHAY HUNTER

9th Grade
Some Years Back

Fourteen-year-old Dixon Wood ran into his high school in a cheerful mood. Although most students dreaded Monday mornings, for Dixon it was the best day of the week, because it meant the weekend was over and he'd get to see his favorite math teacher, Ralph Cram.

Although most children weren't allowed into the building for thirty minutes prior to class, Mr. Cram gave Dixon special privileges, besides he was his little helper.

"Good Morning, Mr. Cram," Dixon said placing his books on the desk as he entered the room. "Can I help you with anything?"

Mr. Cram's smiled brightly at the eager young man standing before him, his white cheeks reddening with emotion like he had for all of his children. "Well I already placed the lessons on the desks, if you want, you can clean the eraser board. But be careful, I don't want you to remove the sign that says Special Guest today."

"No problem," he said excitedly. "Who's coming?"

"You'll see," Mr. Cram replied grinning from ear to ear.

Dixon, always willing to please, jumped at the chance to fulfill his duties. When the board was immaculate, and Mr. Cram sat behind his desk, Dixon approached him. "I'm done, sir, did you need me to do anything else?"

Mr. Cram smiled and said, "I think that's it, son, for now anyway. You can go to your seat and get ready for the surprise I have for you students."

Although Mr. Cram had nothing but adoration and respect for the little boy, Dixon felt otherwise. Mr. Cram was his first crush and he dreamed about him every night his head hit the pillow. In his mind he would imagine what it would be like to kiss him, and for Mr. Cram to say he loved him.

Instead of sitting down Dixon said, "Mr. Cram, I had another bad day at home," he lied. "Can I have another hug?"

In the past, when Dixon was sad, Mr. Cram would honor his request for affection. Although he knew he could lose his job, for touching the children, he took the risk anyway. Anyway, Dixon's home was far from tumultuous. His mother allowed him to do whatever he wanted, and although his father wasn't in her son's life, she made up for it by spoiling him rotten. And as a result, he moved around feeling like everyone and everybody owed him something.

When the students started piling into the classroom, Dixon took a seat in the front row. Once all of the children walked in and were seated, Mr. Cram proudly announced that there would be a visitor, and five minutes later, a beautiful red head woman walked into the room carrying a brand new baby.

"Class, I want to introduce you to my beautiful wife and our two month old son Dillon," he said standing behind her, with his hands on her shoulders.

The class, who was excited for Mr. Cram, all applauded and admired the small infant in her arms. All except Dixon who was brewing with anger.

Who was this bitch to take his man? Ralph belonged to him not her!

Although the other kids were cooing and wooing over the baby, Mr. Cram, noticing that his favorite student hadn't bothered to stand up said, "Dixon, don't you want to see my son?"

Both Mr. Cram and his wife waited for an answer and Dixon responded by leaving the classroom without authorization.

An hour later he returned, but instead of being alone he returned with the police. Mr. Cram's wife was already gone and it was a good thing too, because thanks to Dixon's vicious lies, they arrested him for molestation.

Months later, Mr. Cram did everything he could to disprove the lies, but no one believed him. Everybody, including the staff, recalled how he would allow Dixon into the room after and before school hours. They spoke about the special treatment

Dixon received and before long he was found guilty in a court of law. For the rest of his life Mr. Cram, an honest man, had pedophile stamped on his record and could never outlive the crime.

Oh yes, Dixon could be vicious if he desired, and all those he claimed to care about had better watch out.

SHAY HUNTER

CHAPTER TEN

Charlie

THREE MONTHS LATER

I pull my car up to a big green house in the suburbs of Virginia and park. I had to get another car, because for reasons the mechanic couldn't decipher, it wouldn't work. So with the work I had been getting from Kenny Sugar, I was able to buy an old black Mercedes, which was the most expensive car I ever owned in my life.

Sugar had proven to be a great mentor and friend, and whenever I asked him why he was showing me what he did for a living, he said because it's time to share the knowledge. But I have a feeling that he has another motive, but I doubt he'll ever let me know.

Before getting out of the car, I examine my face in the rearview mirror. Already I was looking like the woman I knew I could be, because thanks to the work Sugar did on me, my cheekbones were higher and I'd lost a little more weight to slim my face and make me appear more feminine. With five thousand dollars saved up already, it was just a matter of time before I could afford the $70,000 needed to get my sex reassignment surgery. Things were finally looking up for me.

Things were going pretty good in my relationship with Nate too. Although I didn't tell him that I was a man, I was able to do things for him to keep him satisfied. Like oral sex, and ass sex when I claimed to be on my period. For now he seems good, but I would hate to think about the day when he'd find out I'm not who he thinks I am.

When I get out of my car and approach the house, I don't get a chance to knock on the door before my client opens it for me. He's a thin brown skin man with high cheekbones and a slender nose. To me he already looks perfect, but I hear people tell me all the time that I don't need work too so I understand.

"Hi, you must be, Gordon," I smile, extending my hand.

"I prefer to be called Gi-Gi," he shakes it softly.

"I understand," I say.

SHAY HUNTER

"It's not a problem," he backs up and allows me inside, "Please come in."

When I walk into his house, it's as beautiful as the homes most gay men keep. Everything smells and looks so clean, it almost looks brand new. He leads me to a room, where a massage bed sits in the middle of the floor.

"Are you a massage therapist?" I sit my doctor's bag on the dresser.

"That's what they call it anyway," he admits, stuffing his hands into his back pockets. "I don't have a license, but I do know how to make my clients feel just as good. It's mostly through jerkoffs and blowjobs though. It really depends on the client. A girl has to make a living."

I nod. "This isn't your first time right?" I ask. "You have gotten butt injections before."

"Actually it is my first time. I heard about you and Sugar's services, and decided to treat myself for my birthday. Why, is it really painful?"

I recall my own experiences and decide to kick shit real with her. "It's the most excruciating thing you probably will ever experience in your life. It will feel like someone is shooting fire under your skin, and you will wonder immediately why you're doing it." I pause to let my words sink in. "By the way, why are you doing it?"

He sighs. "I'm tired of not looking like how I feel on the inside. I'm tired of feeling ugly, when some days I feel pretty. And I'm tired of not getting the attention from the men I find attractive." He shrugs. "I don't know, maybe I want to be someone other than who I am. Do I sound dumb?"

"No, I actually get you because I feel the same way."

She smiles. "Is it true that they call you Tranny 911? When I first heard that term I thought, it's cute and catchy."

"They do call me that, but I'm not sure if I'm cool with the name or not yet. They only say it because I do house calls."

"I think it's cool."

"It's aright, but it damn sure ain't nothing I feel proud of."

"I get it," he laughs. "Well is there anything else I should do to get ready?"

I tell him about the Krazy Glue, about why he needs to massage his butt when I'm done, and I tell him the importance of keeping the procedure a secret. When the instructions are over, I start the procedure and just like everyone else, he sweats and cries.

But when I'm done, I can already tell how pleased he will be with his new ass. Although Kenny gave me his method, after watching him awhile, I found ways to make the technique my own. For instance I use more silicone, and insert more injection

sites, and the result is a rear my girls can be proud
of.

When I'm done he slides on his baggy pants,
per instructions and says, "That was the worst thing I
ever experienced in my life." He exhales.

"I told you it would be," I pack up my bag.

"Yeah, you never lied," he laughs. "But before
you leave aren't you Dixie's roommate?"

I stop packing and look over at him. "Yeah,
why?"

"I'm only asking because I heard something
crazy the other day," he says rubbing his ass.

"Don't do that," I tell him. "Remember what I
said about not altering the cotton balls."

"My bad." His hands drop by his sides.

"But what did you hear?"

"That he killed Old Lady Griselda and her son
in her house."

My eyes widen, and I'm horrified. Until I realize that although Dixie can be a handful, a murderer
he's not. "I think you got the wrong person, Gi-Gi.
You shouldn't believe everything you hear."

He shrugs. "Maybe you're right...I just wanted
you to know."

<hr />

I'm sitting across the table from Nate at Moon
restaurant. When I was with my client, he called to

invite me to dinner. Since it wasn't often that I got invitations to go out with handsome men, I jumped at the opportunity.

Although he looks at me like he wants my body, it always makes me self-conscious about my looks. And no matter how many times I tell him to stop staring at me like I'm a piece of steak, he always ignores my request.

"You know you're sexy as shit right?" he asks.

"Nate, please stop." I look down at my salad and fork the tomatoes.

"Why do I have to stop telling you how I feel?" he reaches across the table and rubs my hand. "You make me feel like I don't have taste or something. Like I don't know beauty when I see it."

"It's not that."

"Then what is it, Charlie?"

"Nate, I don't know, I just don't believe you when you say those types of things sometimes. Because when I look into the mirror, I don't see what you do."

"And that's your problem not mine."

"Where did you come from, Nate? I mean, why do I deserve you?"

"You deserve me 'cause you a good person. And I deserve you 'cause I wanna be happy. Shouldn't that be enough?"

"Enough for who?"

"Us."

SHAY HUNTER

"For some reason, I feel like one day I'm going to wake up and all of this will be a dream. I think if you left me right now, I won't be able to deal. I need you, Nate, and I want to do all that I can to prove it to you."

"And you do," he says.

"Can you make me a promise?" I ask him, putting down my fork.

"Anything."

"If ever you feel like I'm not doing my job. Then you'll let me know? Because I don't want you to hold back anything from—"

When my phone vibrates, and I see Dixie's number on the screen I panic. I forgot that she was making dinner for us tonight. When I was doing my procedure earlier at Gi-Gi's, she called to ask when I was going to be home. I told her in thirty minutes but I forgot all about dinner when Nate called.

"Is everything cool, baby? You look like you just saw a ghost," he says as I look at my phone.

"I have to get home, Nate. I'm so sorry." I stand up and throw my purse over my arm.

"It's not a problem, but what's wrong?"

"In a minute it's going to be everything."

CHAPTER ELEVEN

Dixie

Charlie is standing behind me as I'm throwing pots into the kitchen sink. I swear I feel like laying my hands on her, because of how she's been doing me lately. Although her world is on high right now, I know more about Ms. Charlie's fake ass life than she realizes. If I desire I can shut her down in an instant.

She doesn't take pain as easily as everyone else. If her feelings are hurt, she suffers a nervous breakdown, and that's exactly what I'm going to give her tonight.

"Dixie, can you at least look at me?" Charlie says standing behind me. "I'm so tired of fighting with you!"

"Look at you for what," I turn the water on. "Once again you have made it painfully clear that our friendship doesn't mean anything to you. Which is fucked up because since the day you needed me, I have stood in your corner. I have never, ever left your side, meanwhile you continue to leave mine."

"I know that, but I just lost track of time."

I turn around to face her. "You lost track of time?" I place my hands on my hips. "You went out to dinner with that nigga, when you knew I was making meatloaf at home. That's just wrong, Charlie."

She steps closer to me and I stare into her face. *Her new face.* I hate that life for her seems grand, while mine is at a painful screech. She looks beautiful, like a doll that was popped fresh out of a Barbie box. Her custom-made wig is shiny black, and hangs all the way down her back. A Chinese bang cuts right above her eyes. Her makeup is so flawless, that it doesn't even look like she's wearing any. The red blouse she's wearing opens just a little at the top, revealing her recently injected chest, and her blue jeans hugs her small waist and fat ass. Charlie is bad, and all I'm thinking about is how good it would feel to slash her face in half.

"Dixie, please forgive me." She says. "I got caught up because I'm in love. You know how things are."

When she says she's in love I decide to hit her where it hurts. I walk into the living room and stand next to Nate who is sitting on the sofa. "Who are you in love with, Charlie? Him?" I point in Nate's face.

"Of course." She looks at him. "Who else?"

"You really are green aren't you?"

"What do you mean green?"

"Did you actually think somebody like him, would be with somebody like you on the serious tip?" I giggle. "I mean think about it for a minute because if you do, it will all make sense."

"Dixie, I realize you don't like him, for reasons I don't understand, but he's the right person for me. And if you can't respect that I'm sorry, and that's your business not mine."

"He's married, Charlie," I say cutting her off. "To a beautiful wife who gave him three little girls."

Her eyes widen and she approaches him slowly. "Nate, tell her it's a lie. Tell her you aren't married."

"He doesn't have to tell me anything, because I'm letting you know what the case is. That's what I'm talking about, you never listen to me, even though I'm in your corner. This man that you chose over your friend does not belong to you and he never will."

"Nate, tell her it's a lie," Charlie says to him. "Tell her you aren't married."

Tears pour out of her eyes and it's almost too pathetic to watch. But truth be told she deserves everything she's getting right now. Charlie is starting to feel herself and it's time she be busted down. All the way down.

"Baby, open your mouth and give me the respect I deserve," Charlie continues. "You hear her talking that shit. So tell her you aren't married!"

He holds his head down. "I'm sorry, Charlie, I really am, I can't do that. He's right."

Her jaw drops and she stands in the middle of the living room floor as stiff as a mannequin.

"That's what I wanted to tell you earlier, but I figured you wouldn't want to know because you couldn't handle it. I care about you, Charlie. I'm not like mothafuckas like him. I actually care about you and your feelings, but this nigga doesn't."

"You going too far now, Dixie," Nate says.

"I'm telling the truth and you know it." I walk up to Charlie and massage her shoulders. "You deserve better than him, and one day, you'll get it. Now I'm sorry it had to come out like this, but I didn't know what else to do. You were becoming a different person with him, Charlie."

"I...I can't take this." She grabs her purse and rushes away.

"Where are you going?" I ask walking behind her.

"I can't be in here right now. I gotta...I gotta leave." She walks out of the door, slamming it behind her.

When she's gone Nate says, "Was all that necessary, Dixon? I mean really."

"Whatever, nigga, don't act like you didn't know what the deal was when all this shit started. So stop the guilt trip right where it is."

"I did, I mean, I knew you were going to hurt his feelings, but did you have to be so hard on him?"

I step up to him and look into his eyes. "Are you telling me, that you fell in love with him? Are you telling me that you were actually serious, and wanted to be in a relationship? And if your answer is yes, what were you going to do with your wife?"

"Of course I don't love her," he stands up and stuffs his hands into his pockets. "I mean, I just didn't think you would shoot her down like that, that's all. I thought you would've been a little easier, since she's your friend. I mean, ya'll may have your beef, but I spent enough time with her to know she cares about you."

"You don't know shit about me or Charlie, bitch. You ain't nothing but a washed up nigga on crack." He walks up to me like he's going to hurt me. "Don't even try it, Nate. You know about me. My name rings in the streets. Please don't make a mistake of letting the government job fool you. I'm a slayer...believe that shit."

SHAY HUNTER

He backs down. "Where the fuck is my money?" he asks.

I grin and walk over to my purse on the counter. I take out five hundred dollars and hand them to him. "That's everything I agreed to pay you."

"One day you gonna get what's coming to you," he tucks the money into his back pocket.

"And what the fuck is that supposed to mean?"

"My wife told me what kind of person you are, Dixon. She told me you can't be trusted, and how her co-worker went to lunch with you, and that's the last time anybody saw her alive. I heard a lot of crazy shit, but now I'm seeing what she means."

"And what about you? What about how you came to the job six months ago to pick her up, only to slide away to give me your number. What about how I had you sucking this dick like it was going out of style. Please miss me with the foolery, Nate. I'm guilty as charged, and you're my co-defendant."

He frowns. "Whatever, I'm out of here."

Before he reaches the door I say, "I take it that this is our little secret. If I even think that you are going to tell Charlie about how I hired you to break his heart, I will personally ruin your world."

Fortunately for him he leaves without another word.

CHAPTER TWELVE

Charlie

I'm sitting at a straight bar, alone drinking my heart away. I can't believe that just hours earlier, I was on top of the world when Nate was in my life, and now I'm at the bottom. Maybe I deserve to have this type of pain right now, considering I never told him about me being a man. But how could I?

I saw how he looked at other women, when we were out on the street. I saw the stares they gave him, and the ones he returned. The last thing I needed was to tell him I was a man, when in actuality I am a female stuck in the wrong body. When I know I'm going to have the surgery, just as soon as I can raise the money.

SHAY HUNTER

While I'm drinking a glass of wine, a handsome familiar face comes in and sits about five seats down from me at the bar. I can't remember where I saw him before and it doesn't matter anyway, because I'm done with men.

After my fifth glass of wine, when I feel someone staring at me, I glance down. It's the same man I recognized, but couldn't remember from where. When I look at his brown eyes, and his muscular arms under his black shirt, I know I have to leave, before I get my hopes up high as usual.

So I pay my check and make my exit toward the door. Although I make it to my car, I have no idea where I'm going. I can't go home right now, because I can't face Dixie.

Besides, all she wanted to do was look out for me, and what did I do? Choose a nigga over her. And it's not even like I meant to do it on purpose, even though it was done all the same. It's just that Nate made me feel good and I needed him to bring me happiness. I actually made it his responsibility.

When I reach the light, and look out of my rearview mirror, I see the same eyes staring at me from the bar, inside the car behind me. He flashes his lights and I take off, before the light even turns green. I hope he's not trying to get my attention because I'm not interested.

But when I reach another light, he pulls up on the driver's side in his silver Lexus. "Are you running away from me?" he asks. "Cause if you are, you hurting my feelings."

"I'm married," I respond rolling my eyes. "I'm not even interested."

"That's funny," he says slyly.

"And why is that?" I focus back on the light, and wonder why it hasn't turned green yet.

"Because I've been staring at you for over an hour, and I didn't see a ring on that finger. And trust me, I looked."

"It don't matter if you saw a ring or not, because I'm taken anyway." When the light turns again, I take off so fast my wheels screech, and leave a cloud of dust behind me. But as luck would have it, he catches me at the next light, and pulls up next to me again.

"Let me take you out to dinner, gorgeous. I promise it will be no strings attached. Cross my heart and hope to die." He raises his hands in the air.

"I'm not interested," I roll my eyes and focus back on the road.

"You have to be," he says. "You were looking at me as much as I was looking at you back at the bar. Before you say no let me make something clear. You should know that when I see something that belongs to me, I take it."

I frown. "Don't nothing over here belong to you."

SHAY HUNTER

"Are you sure about that? Because if you ask me, I see my future wife."

I roll my eyes. "You can try that tired ass line on somebody else if you want to, but I'm not buying it."

Although I tell him I'm not interested, something about his bossiness makes me want him even more. But I have a history of picking the wrong men, so I must avoid him at all costs. I have too!

When the light turns green I pull off again. And when he follows me, I grab my cell phone out of my purse. Then I show it to him when we reach another light. "If you don't stop following me, I'm calling the police. I'm not fucking around with you."

"Okay, okay, let's do this," he says, totally unmoved. "Let me take you out on one date." He raises one finger. "And if you don't like me after that, I'll call the police on myself. I'll say that I'm harassing you, and that I need to be locked up immediately." I smile. "Come on, beautiful. Don't make me wait too much longer. We don't have any more stop lights left after this."

I'm not going to lie, it feels good to be pursued like this. Before I give him my answer, I look into his eyes. Something about him feels right so I read him my number.

When the light turns green he says, "Wait, what's the area code?"

"If you really want me you'll find it." I pull off, and eye him in the rear view mirror. He's smiling the entire time.

SHAY HUNTER

CHAPTER THIRTEEN

Charlie

"This is what you'll need for some of my customers. I don't like to give it to them too much, because it causes them to be drowsy, but it works," Sugar says showing me a medicine bottle within the closet at his house.

"Why not give it to everybody then? They can never take the pain."

"Because I prefer that customers don't go to sleep. The last thing we need is someone passing out, and dying on the table, because I put them under." He says. "I only have four people I give it to, and that's only because they're so loud when I inject them that I can't concentrate. They are my highest paying customers and the money is worth the risk, because I know they'll take my secret to their grave if something went wrong. The last thing they want is somebody knowing they were getting butt injections."

I laugh. "What's that bottle right there?" I point to a red pill bottle that isn't labeled.

"Something I use to get back at people who deserve it." He closes the closet. "I'll leave it like that for now."

I giggle and then he coughs harshly. He had been doing that for a while, and whenever I ask him what's going on, and if he's okay, he shakes me off.

When he walks to the bedroom, I decide to follow him inside. "Sugar, what's going on with the cough? And before you tell me nothing, please understand that I'm going to keep asking until you tell me the truth."

He eases into bed and climbs under the sheets. "I told you not to worry about me, Charlie. Focus on yourself, and what you want out of life. Your energy will be better spent that way."

"I'm not going for that this time, Sugar. How come you won't let me be there for you? Whenever I need you you're there, but how come you won't let me return the favor?"

"Charlie, I have AIDS."

He looks into my eyes and I try to pretend that the news he gave me isn't devastating. I try to act as if I'm not scared for him, and worried that I won't get to know him better.

SHAY HUNTER

I swallow and sit on the edge of the bed. It squeaks a little. "Why didn't you tell me before, Sugar? I knew something was up with you."

He shrugs. "To tell you the truth, I haven't told the people I spend most of my time with either." He sighs. "I guess I don't like people fussing over me. Anyway, how many people do you know with HIV? It's so common now it doesn't warrant a pity party anymore. I just want to live the last few days of my life in peace."

"But I know people who have it, who are so healthy you'd never know. What's going on with you? What's different?"

"I didn't take the medicine."

"But why?" I yell, moving closer to the head of the bed. "You could live a long life with the meds, Sugar. Why wouldn't you do what you need for your body?"

"My mother died five years ago. She was the most beautiful woman in the world, Charlie. The kind of woman they don't make anymore and I've missed her for every second that she's been gone. I want to see her again, and if this is the only way that I can do it, then so be it."

I'm so angry right now I'm shaking. Who is he to come into my life, make me love him, only to prove to be a weakling? If I told him how many days I wanted to die, and take my own life when things didn't go my way, he'd probably never believe me.

"I think you're wrong for this, Sugar. You could live if you really wanted to, but you don't. That's some selfish ass shit."

"I'm just choosing to die, Charlie," he touches my hand softly. "That's the difference. And if you love me, you'll respect my decision."

"I'll never respect it," I say softly. As I look at him things suddenly make sense. "This is really why you taught me how to do the procedures. You're dying, and you wanted someone else to carry out your name."

"If that's what you call it."

I stand up and walk toward his dresser. "Now what?"

"For starters you'll live your life, Charlie. You'll save the money you need for your procedure and you get out of the business. Don't stay in it too long because you'll get caught. And then you get away from Dixie."

I roll my eyes. "I don't feel like talking about him again, Sugar."

"Well I do. Like I've been telling you for months, I don't trust Dixie, Charlie. And I've spent so much time trying to explain to you how important it is to move, that I'm starting to get blue in the face. That dude is dangerous."

"Dixie might have his shit with him, but he has always looked out for me. It was because of him that

I found out that Nate was married, instead of wasting the rest of my life."

"Yeah, and I wonder how he knew that."

"What are you trying to say?"

"Ms. Sugar ain't *trying* to say anything. I made myself clear. If I were you, I'd snatch away a little piece of my savings, get a place and leave. I certainly wouldn't live in that man's house, or have him around my new friend. Speaking of your new man toy, how are things going between you two?"

"Slow, but I like it like that," I smile, just thinking about him. "He's doing all the right things and I'm kind of nervous."

Luke Crow had proven to be a perfect gentlemen, and it was because of him I wanted to get my sexual reassignment surgery so that when we finally made love, he would be able to experience it with the woman he's interested in, not the man I am physically.

"Good, which is even more reason for you to take your man and bounce."

"What exactly do you think Dixie has done that warrants me to leave?"

"For starters I think he murdered Griselda and her son. People in the neighborhood are saying he was dealing with her on the side. But when they examined her body, she had showered prior to her death, so there wasn't anything left behind."

"First off Dixie likes men."

"First off Dixie will fuck anything that moves," he says to me, before coughing. "I know you not dumb enough to believe anything different."

"Dixie is my friend, Sugar."

"And I am your friend too, Charlie. Please, leave that house now, before he ruins the rest of your life."

I walk back over to the bed, and sit down. "If I work to get out of the house, will you take the medicines you're supposed to manage your condition?"

"So you blackmailing me now?"

"If that's what you call it."

He sighs and then looks up at the ceiling. "Let's make a deal, you work to get out of that house, and I'll do better with my health. Deal?"

I grin. "Deal."

SHAY HUNTER

CHAPTER FOURTEEN

Charlie

I can't lie, after speaking to Sugar the other day, I was starting to wonder about who Dixie really is. And part of me hated it, because although we had our problems, he had always been there for me and I couldn't see him the way that Sugar did. And as far as murder I can't imagine, because even at his worst, he couldn't be capable of something so foul.

I was almost home when my phone rang. It was Luke. I quickly answered like I always did whenever he called. Smiling a little wider than I wanted I said, "Hey, you I was just thinking about you."

"Listen at you running game," he says. "You always talking about me spooning you lines and here you are kicking game to me. You not gonna swell up my head and start having me believe all of that shit."

"I'm serious, Luke, I was just thinking about you," I say honestly. I drive slowly, so that I can stay on the phone with him longer.

"Well if you're really thinking about me, why don't you come over my house? It seems like if I don't see you in a restaurant or a movie theater, I'm not seeing you at all. You know I don't have a problem wining and dining you, but I'm looking for some next level shit."

"I wish I could, but Dixie hasn't been feeling too well lately, and I wanted to check up on her, and make sure she's okay before I do anything."

I hear him sigh loudly.

"What's wrong, Luke?"

"You don't really want to know what's wrong with me," he says in an irritated tone.

"I do."

"It's a lot of things, but I'll start with what's bugging me the most. How come I haven't been to your house yet, Charlie? It's not like I haven't asked several times to come over, and every time I do, you giving me the run around. I mean, you ashamed of me or something?"

"No, I mean, you know that's not true." I can't imagine remotely being embarrassed of him. He's the most attractive man I ever dated in my life. If anything I want the world to know he's mine, and I'm his."

"I don't know shit. All I know is that I'm trying to get to know my future wife better, and she's not meeting me half way. So you tell me now, are you trying to be serious about me or am I wasting my time?"

"You know I'm serious, Luke. And if I'm giving you any other impression I'm so sorry."

"I don't know shit except that every time I invite you over here, or try to go over your house, there's a problem. You say you got a roommate but how do I know it's not another nigga?"

That's the thing about lies. After awhile they get you so wrapped up in them, that you don't know what's real or fake anymore. I didn't want to bring him home because I didn't want Dixie ruining it for me. I didn't want Dixie to be jealous that I had a new friend, and I didn't want Dixie to think that I was disloyal just for spending time with him.

Although Dixie said he didn't care about me being in a relationship, it always seemed as if strange things happened whenever I met someone new. And now, I'm tired of being alone. I want someone to love me and hold me, and if that's a problem, then maybe Sugar is right. Maybe it is time for me to move on.

"Luke, what can I do to show you I'm true? Say the word and it's done, baby."

"Invite me to your home."

My heart feels like it dropped in my high heels. If I say no he'll be frustrated, but if I say yes, Dixie will undoubtedly ruin things for me. Dixie is not exactly a people person, and although she claims people like her, most people don't.

"Okay, Luke," I relent, looking at the road ahead of me. "If that's what I have to do, that's what I'll do."

"What exactly are you saying?" he asks.

"I'm saying you can come to my house, because there is no way I'm going to allow something so petty to come between us. It's too early for all of that."

"Don't play with me, baby, I don't know if I ever told you before, but I don't like games."

"I'm serious, Luke," I giggled. "I want you to trust me, and if you think I'm hiding something, that'll cause problems with us, I want it addressed immediately."

"That's what I'm talking about, baby girl. Honesty. That kind of thing will make us go so far. Never, ever lie to me about anything. That's the only way you can break the bond we build together."

"I know, I know," I say. "But look, I need to tell you about my roommate before we do anything. I want you to be prepared."

"He's a guy right?"

"Yes."

"You fucking him?" he says with an attitude.

"No, Luke, it's nothing like that."

He seems relieved. "So if you not fucking him what's the problem?"

"He's gay," I say softly. "Like real flamboyant and loud."

"So he's a faggy?"

My stomach churns. If he thinks Dixon's the only faggy in the building he'll have a problem when he learns about me. "What do you mean?"

"Is he the type of nigga who's always making a bunch of noise so that everybody can see him?"

"Yes, but will that make you look differently at me?"

"I'm going to put it like this, since I got with you, baby, you've been nothing but classy. And as long as you don't change who you are when you're in his presence, then I'm going to like you the same."

"Are you sure? Because if you leave me right now, I'm going to die, Luke. I've had some bad things happen to me in the past, and I'm looking for a little change now."

"Never leaving you, baby." he chuckles. "But if you are that worried about your friend, then he must be a mess. Am I right?

"You just gonna have to meet him yourself," I say pulling up to the house.

"I got you, mami. Just shoot me the address and I'm on my way."

Tranny 911

Luke and I are sitting on the sofa, watching Dixie do the most as she struts around the house barely clothed. I'm leaning against his side, and he has his arm behind me, with his hand rubbing my shoulder. And instead of enjoying the moment, I'm fuming mad at the way Dixie is behaving. Damn I just wish he could act regular just the one time.

For instance I can't believe what Dixie chose to put on tonight. I told him I was having company, and instead of him being decent, he's wearing a pair of black tights that showcases his dick bulging, along with a red bra even though he has no titties inside. What the fuck is wrong with him?

"Please excuse me, Luke, I didn't know you were coming until you were outside and I feel bad about what I'm wearing." he runs his hand down his thighs. "I would've put on something a little more presentable, had I known. But this is how I walk around the house."

I can't believe he just sat up here and lied. Not only did I tell him Luke was coming, I told him to put on something nice because I didn't want my man to feel uncomfortable. Days like this make me think that maybe Sugar is on to him. Maybe he is a hater.

"You can still go in the back and put something different on you know," Luke tells him. "I mean it ain't like you not at your own crib."

SHAY HUNTER

"Am I making you uncomfortable?" Dixie replies batting his non-existent eyelashes.

You making me uncomfortable, bitch. I think.

"I would like to get to know you, since my girl speaks so highly of you and all. But if I'm being honest I will say that the sequin bra you freaking is a little distracting."

Dixie's forehead wrinkles and she seems highly offended. "What you trying to say?"

"Your outfit is loud," Luke continues. "You supposed to rock something like that for the one you with. Feel me? I'm not trying to see all of that right now."

He frowns a little. "They're just clothes, Luke, I mean my body doesn't intimidate you does it?"

"It's not about that, shawty," Luke continues. "I'm all the way good over here and I never get intimidated. And in case you haven't noticed, my wife is bad as shit so there's no need for me to look at anything else."

Dixie frowns and I swear I can see a tinge of jealousy. "Your wife huh?"

"Yes, my wife," he kisses me on the cheek.

Dixie stares at me. She's giving me a look that I understand all too well. She's asking me, without opening her mouth, if I think he'll be okay once he learns that the woman he chose to hang by his side is actually a man. Why can't he just let me be happy, whether he likes my decisions or not.

"It must be good to have someone to hold you down," Dixie replies, looking at Luke. "And you seem to be holding her pretty tight."

"It feels great," Luke grins.

"So I guess ya'll gonna have kids and everything huh?" Dixie continues.

What is he doing? He knows that I can't have kids.

"If she wants to have kids we will, if she doesn't I'm good with that too. I'm just trying to figure out what this has to do with you putting on clothes."

I'm about to shit on myself when suddenly my phone rings. It's my client and I stand up, walk towards the hallway and answer the call. "I'm kind of busy right now, Gi-Gi. You mind if I call you back later?"

"I need to see you right now, Charlie. It's urgent."

I sigh. "What's so important that it can't wait until later?" I look over at Luke and he blows a kiss at me softly.

"I went to the doctor's today."

The moment he says that, my heart beats rapidly. If there is one thing that Sugar and I are scared of more than the devil himself, is the doctor. Because although our clients know that what we do is illegal, when faced with either dying, or telling the doctor what was pushed into their bodies, to cause them to be sick, they will likely point fingers our way.

"So...so what did the doctor say?" I ask. Although I'm scared as hell, I can't be too loud because Luke thinks I'm a nurse, and he has no idea about my illegal lifestyle.

"He says I have an infection. But that's not why I'm calling you."

"What is it?"

"You have to come see me right now. Something is going on with my injection site. Everything you did fell to the back of my legs and I need you to repair it. You gotta come now, Charlie."

CHAPTER FIFTEEN

Charlie

My hands are shaking the entire way as I walk toward Gi-Gi's house. I don't know what I'm supposed to do in the event that a patient gets hurt, or infected with a procedure. Outside of telling them that whatever happens, they shouldn't tell the doctor, I don't know what else to say. And when I called Sugar earlier to find out the process for something like this, I was told by Sunshine that he was taken to the hospital. So on top of all of this, now I have to worry about him too.

When I make it to Gi-Gi's house, I walk inside without knocking. "Gi-Gi, I'm here, where are you?" I ask walking towards the back. "Gi-Gi, I'm here."

In a real weak voice she says, "I'm here, Charlie. In the back. In my bedroom."

SHAY HUNTER

I quickly move for the bedroom and when I open the door, I see him lying in the bed with a white sheet up to his neck. I never knew a black person's skin could turn blue yet here I was looking at Gi-Gi's altered state. So much sweat was running down his face, that it poured from his scalp.

Slowly I walk over to him, still not knowing what to say or do. "Gi-Gi, what happened to you?"

"I told you already, I have an infection."

"I know but...what...I mean why is it hitting you this bad?"

"I don't know, one minute I was massaging a client and the next minute my butt started burning a lot. Pus was pouring out of my flesh, dampening my pants and it started hurting worse than it did when you gave me the injections. But like I said on the phone, that's not why I called you over here."

"Then what is?" I ask trembling.

"Some of the silicone slid down to the back of my thighs in knots, and I need you to do something about it. I can't walk around like this, Charlie. I would never be able to live with myself."

"Gi-Gi, I know it probably looks awful right now. And I know you paid for a service and deserve to be able to take advantage of it. But the last thing you need to be worried about right now is more injections. What did the doctor say?"

"He told me I have MRSA."

"What is that?"

"It's called Methicillin-Resistant Staph Airy something. I couldn't remember the entire thing he said, but I think that's close."

"Did he tell you what caused it?"

"No, but I'm sure it has something to do with the silicone. A friend of mine had the same thing after she got injections, but now she's doing fine. I'm taking antibiotics so it's cool, and I don't want you to worry about anything. Like I said, that's not the reason I want you here."

The next question I don't want to know, but I have to ask anyway. "Did you tell him about me? And the procedures?"

"No, I would never do that. Unless—"

A short jolt of uneasiness pierces my stomach. "Unless what?"

"Unless you don't fix what you did to me. I requested butt injections, and now I have a problem I didn't see coming. I know it's wrong to blackmail you but you leave me know other choice. When I tried to come at you on some serious shit on the phone, you didn't accept. Talking about I needed to get better first."

"It's not that I didn't accept it, Gi-Gi, it's that I'm worried about your health." I sit in a chair across from the bed. "If you want me to come back later, when you're feeling better to do whatever I can for your legs, then I will. I'll even have Sugar come over with me, so that we can find out what's going on. I just want you to heal first."

"Today, Charlie. Not tomorrow, next week, or the month after that. I want this problem gone today."

There was no way I was going to stick him with any more silicone, or poke at the silicone in the back of his legs. I don't give a fuck what he says. It's bad enough that he's doing badly. What I look like adding to the problem, by giving him more of what caused it? I can't do it.

"I'm sorry I can't—"

All of a sudden Gi-Gi starts shaking so hard the bed rattles. His eyes roll to the back of his head, and foam oozes from the corners of his mouth. I immediately hop up and move toward him, not sure what I'm going to do now. After all, I'm a fake surgeon not a doctor. He's having some sort of seizure and I don't know what to do.

"Gi-Gi, what's going on," I scream looking him up and down. I feel so useless. "Talk to me! Please!"

My request doesn't reach him because he can't talk. He seems unconscious. And then, suddenly the trembling dies down, like a blender being turned off. He looks at me with wide eyes, and then his eyes roll to the back of his head and his lids slam shut.

"Gi-Gi," I yell touching his throat. "Gi-Gi, please wake up, don't do this shit to me."

Tranny 911

When I finally calm down, I try and feel for the pulse that's needed for him to be alive. It isn't there! He can't be dead! I didn't sign up for this shit. I drop to the floor, as I try desperately to get my mind in order. Pain rushes up my lower back to my neck because of how I landed on the floor. What am I going to do now?

I crawl over to my purse and dial Sugar's number. I know he's in the hospital, but I'm hoping to get in contact with his assistant again. Maybe he can talk to me, and tell me what to do next. But there was no answer.

Quickly I weigh my options. If I call the cops, they will want to investigate me. Before long I'm sure they'll find out that I was the one who injected him, and maybe I'll be wanted for murder. I can't let that happen. I can't go to jail. There is only one thing left to do.

I have to call Dixie.

We are on Dixie's grandmother's property, somewhere out Virginia. The moon in the purple sky gives us just enough light to dispose of our problem. Dirt covers my face and hands, compliments of a hard night's work. Dixie has the shovel in his hand, and he is hitting the pile of dirt where Gi-Gi's body rests underneath the earth.

SHAY HUNTER

I'm consumed with guilt but I sincerely didn't see any other option to dispose of Gi-Gi's body. I can't go to jail for the rest of my life, just because of one mistake. I just can't. If that makes me selfish I guess I'll have to answer to my God later, and pray for forgiveness.

"You okay, Charlie?" he asks throwing the shovel on the ground.

"You know that I'm not," I say softly, looking at the freshly pressed grave.

He walks over to me and pulls me toward him. I can smell the sweet stink of the sweat rolling from his underarms. But even with all of that, under his embrace I feel safe. So I let it all go. I cry hard, and now that I think about it, probably harder than I had in my entire life.

When I'm done I separate from him and look at his freckly face. "What now?"

He sighs. "What you mean? We move on. We forget about this and never say a word to anyone."

I look at his grandmother's old house behind him. It's a beaten down wooden house that leans slightly to the right. "Anybody live here anymore?"

He laughs. "Nobody lives here. The property was left to me as a chow, and I don't know what to do with it so I kept it around. Grandma was the one person in the world who loved me. And when she died, I wanted to keep something to remember her. Sometimes when I come here, I sit in her house and just think." He looks at the house and I see a tear fall down his eyes. "I think about her a lot, and wonder if she's mad at me, for the choices I made in my life."

In all of the time I hung with him, I never saw him cry real tears. He'd go through the motions, but no water ever left his eyes until now.

"Thank you for helping me, Dixie."

"Girl, please," he laughs. "You know I have your back."

"I know, but this is on another level."

"And you called the right person. This is what I'm talking about, when I tell you how unbreakable our bond is. You think you could trust Sugar with this type of information, or Luke?"

I shake my head. "I don't know."

"Of course you couldn't, Charlie. Sooner or later you're going to realize that the only one you can trust in this world is me."

I wonder if that's true.

"I'll never leave your side. Besides, I been taking care of you for too long now."

"But you shouldn't have to."

"But I love to," Dixie yells louder. "I love taking care of you."

"I know you do," I say not wanting to argue anymore. "And one day I'm going to be able to return the favor and take care of you too."

SHAY HUNTER

"Well I can't wait for that day," he jokes. "Old girl is due for some love." He pauses. "So are you going to tell Sugar about what happened?"

"I'm not going to tell anybody. Besides, I still need this job to make money."

"You know at first I wasn't with it, but now I think that's a smart choice to keep this on the low. Don't let nobody stop your paper flow, not even the dead bitch currently in her grave."

CHAPTER SIXTEEN

Dixie

My boss got on my motherfucking nerves today. I knew I was going to have a bad day the moment I woke up and heard Charlie on the phone talking to Luke. They act like they can't spend five minutes without talking on the phone to each other, and she doesn't have any respect for other people living in the house. The least she could do is keep her voice down.

Anyway today at work my boss tells me at the last minute that there would be a meeting. That's all well and dandy, but the meeting was during my lunch break and I wasn't about to postpone what I planned just to attend it. I was meeting Fergie who was letting me borrow one of her wigs for a show that day. So when I told him I wasn't coming, he

SHAY HUNTER

wrote me up for insubordination and gave me a warning. Since I already have some marks on my record for calling out dick, if I get in trouble one more time, I'll be suspended. I hate that fucking job!

When I park my car and walk into my house, I'm irritated when I smell a strong scent of cologne. Sure enough when I bend the corner, Luke is sitting on *my* sofa, with Charlie lying on his lap while they're watching TV.

"Hey, Dixie," Charlie says to me. "How was your day at work? I called earlier to tell you Luke was coming over."

"I don't want to talk about it right now."

"Well did you see this movie? We can start it over if you want, it's only been on for fifteen minutes."

"What movie," I say with an attitude, as I toss my purse on the counter.

"Django, with Jamie Foxx? Girl he killed the damn thing. I been meaning to see this for a minute and Luke brought it over."

I look at Luke, who hasn't bothered to say shit to me since I stepped inside. This is my fucking house, not his. "Must be nice," I sigh. "Unfortunately I couldn't sit at home and watch no movie because I had to work," I say opening the refrigerator. "In case you haven't realized it, I am gainfully employed."

Charlie looks at me, but then lies back on his lap. She doesn't bother to say anything.

Tranny 911

"You aight," Luke asks. "Cause you seem like you got a lot on your shoulders from where I'm sitting over here."

Even though I can't stand him, I understand why Charlie likes him so much. Physically he's the sexiest man I ever seen in my life. Not only are the tattoos that appear to cover his entire body hot, he is tall and built like a gladiator. Still, the nigga is infamous for jumping in my business when it comes to Charlie and if truth be told, I'm tired of it.

"Why wouldn't everything be alright?" I ask him. "The world is mine, boo didn't you know?"

"Naw," he chuckles. "I ain't get that memo."

"Well you should stay informed, sweetie," I respond. "Because it's very true."

"Just leave Dixie alone," Charlie says to him. "She probably had a bad day at work."

"Him," Luke responds focusing back on the TV.

"What you talking about baby?" Charlie asks.

"You said she and I'm tired of you doing that. Dixie is a man not a woman. As far as I'm concerned nothing about him is lady like. I just want you to use correct terms when you speaking about him, in case you say the wrong thing out on the streets."

"Why don't you like me," I ask walking into the living room. "Let's just put the shit out on the table right now." I fold my arms over my chest. "I'm listening."

"Who said I didn't like you?"

"Baby, let's just watch the movie," Charlie says softly. "Please. I just want to enjoy this time with you without all the drama."

"Don't you see we're having a conversation, Charlie? Besides, there's no drama when the truth is involved." I look at Luke. "Let's put the shit on the line right now so we can figure out what's going on. Because I got a feeling that you don't like me because you always coming out your neck sideways." I frown and place my hands on my hips.

"And just how does one talk out the side of their neck?"

"For starters whenever you come home, and we in here, you fussing and arguing with my girl. I get the impression that ain't nothing good going on in your life, and you try to take it out on everybody else."

Charlie sits up straight, and lowers her head.

Yes, darling. The shit has hit the fan now.

"Nigga, you may be over here roping Charlie's mind, but you can't even begin to know what's going on in my head. Never am I jealous or taking my problems out on anyone. You got me all the way fucked up, sweetie pie."

"I don't gotta be in your head," he continues. "It's evident how you think. It's all in how you carry yourself. Every time I see you it's like all you got is a bunch of troubles. Relax."

I laugh. "Who the fuck died and made you God?"

"There you go talking that slick shit again. If we going to have a conversation, then let's have a conversation. You can leave that fly shit for them fuckin' faggies you roll with. I'm not interested."

I look at Charlie and she's trembling. She knows how I am and she realizes that it's just a matter of time before I read this mothafucka. I can't believe that this nigga is really sitting up in here, in my house, talking about faggies. He has no idea that the female he is currently bunned up with, is a member of the faggy crew. What a fucking idiot! I can ruin her whole world if I desire to and I'm seriously contemplating it.

"If only you knew," I smirk.

"Please, Dixie, don't do this," Charlie says to me. "I'm begging you."

"If only I knew what," he asks me. "What he talking about, baby?" He looks at Charlie but she doesn't respond. So he focuses back on me. "Don't bite your tongue now, Dixon. Just come out and say it."

"If I told you what was on my mind right now, trust me, you'd never be able to handle it."

"I can handle anything, my nigga. Anything you throw my way."

SHAY HUNTER

"Are you sure about that?"
"Positive."
I look at Charlie again. "Well here goes…"

CHAPTER SEVENTEEN

Dixie

When I went to work today, I was brought in an office and fired. All because I called out the day before yesterday. I know I could've went to work, but I didn't feel like it. After Luke started talking dumb shit, I got so upset that I went out drinking with Fergie later on that night. It has been a long time since someone rubbed me raw like that.

And even though I could've told him that the bitch he held so dear to his heart, is actually Charles Monroe, I kept the secret. For now anyway.

I'm laying on my bed getting my dick sucked by Eddie from up the street. Although he claimed he wasn't gay, and didn't like to take dick or fuck me in the ass, he loved to suck my dick while he jerked off.

So while my dick was in his mouth, I held a conversation on the phone with my bitch.

"You sure you okay, girl," Fergie asks me. "Because you sounded mad as shit when I called earlier today. I was about to come over but you didn't tell me where you were."

"I just lost my job, Fergie. Why would I be okay?"

"I know you shouldn't be okay, I didn't mean it that way, you know that. I was asking if you were better that's all."

When Eddie starts sucking my dick better, I felt myself stiffening up. "I'll be good in a minute." I tell her allowing the tingling sensation to take over my body. "But anyway, what's up with you? You don't call me back to back like this unless you want something. And don't tell me you wanted to see how I was doing because I know that's not the case."

"That's a fucking lie."

"Fergie, cut the shit. You know I've been knowing you for too long. Now either tell me what's up or I'm getting off of the phone. Anyway I'm busy right now."

"Okay, okay, bitch, don't hang up or fake drop the cell phone call. I know you gonna get mad but I need to know…where is Charlie?"

"Please don't tell me you're on Charlie's dick too," I say pushing into Eddie's face.

"It ain't even like that," she sighs.

Tranny 911

"Then what's it like?"

"I want some work done, and I wanted to make an appointment with her. I had her number but for whatever reason, I can't find it right now."

When Eddie's mouth gets wetter I say, "Give me a second, Fergie."

I place the phone down on the side of the bed, and grab the top of his head. Then I push into his mouth ten to twelve times, until my nut squeezes out and oozes out onto his tongue. It feels so good, that my entire body vibrates and I bite down on my lip. And when I look down at him, I see his dick shoots out cream all over my gray bedspread.

Never one for a bunch of words, he wipes his mouth and says, "Thanks, man." He stands up, drops fifty bucks on the table and pulls his pants up. "I get up with you later."

"No doubt."

When he walks out of my room, and I hear the front door close I pick up the phone. "Now what were you saying about Charlie's whore ass again?"

"Please don't tell me you had me on hold, while you were getting your dick sucked. Please tell me you not that rancid."

"Bitch, you called *me* when he was over here. Instead of telling you to call back like I had ten times already today, I decided to talk to you and see what the fuck you wanted. Even though up to this point, I still haven't found out. Now stop playing games and tell me the deal. Why you calling so much?"

"I need to make an appointment with Charlie. I need work girl, and I need it like yesterday."

"What you getting?"

"Butt injections. You know I use to go to Sugar, but she been sick lately and the word on the street is she's stop taking clients. And whatever is wrong with her, I heard that doctors don't think she's going to make it."

"It serves her ass right. Maybe when she's dead she'll learn to stay out of my business."

"That's cold, Dixie."

"It may be cold but it's the truth. Since that bitch entered my life she has done nothing but try to tear my friendship apart with Charlie."

"I don't know about all that, Dixie, but I hear Sugar is good people."

"You can believe that if you want to, but you should know Sugar's murdering ass killed somebody. Now do you still think she's so sweet?"

"What you talking 'bout," Fergie asked. "Who she kill?"

"Remember Gordon?"

"You talking about pretty Gi-Gi. The one who did the massages?"

"Yeah, she killed him. Haven't you heard, he's been missing for months now, and nobody can find him. That's because Sugar did some wrong shit and got rid of the body. I overheard Charlie talking to Sugar about it on the phone and everything."

"Oh my, God, Dixie. That girl has family and everything. I think she was even getting ready to adopt a baby! I can't believe it."

"Believe it because it's true. Sugar not the saint everybody makes her out to be. She most certainly has her shit with her, and when people realize that they'll stop putting folks on thrones."

"Wow, thanks for the 'T' but anyway, I need to get up with Charlie."

"First off you know Charlie charges $1,500 for her procedures, and me and you both know you not sitting on that much money right now."

"I know, but I was hoping she'd give me a discount, seeing as though we friends and all."

"Charlie about her money. Trust me when I say she ain't giving no breaks or handouts, Fergie. You gonna either have to raise the money or she not fucking with you."

"You sure, girl?"

"I tell no lies," she responds.

"Then what I'm going to do?" she sighs. "I'm so sick of my ass and hips that I don't know what to do with it."

"Well luckily for you, I have a plan. Now you know I do the procedures too right? Sugar taught Charlie and he taught me."

Now I know I've never done them before, but I went with Charlie a few times after we buried Gi-Gi. He wanted me there for support. But whenever I went with him, I always paid attention to everything he doing. Shit, it ain't like Charlie had official schooling in injections, or even Sugar for that matter. And I feel confident that if they can do it, I can too. Besides, since I am unemployed, I need the money.

"I didn't know you did them," she says excitedly. "Bitch, why you just telling me now. As much as I be talking about getting pumped."

"Bitch, yes, and I don't charge as much as Charlie does either. You can get mine for five hundred dollars a procedure."

"Why so cheap?" she asks suspiciously.

"Because I'm building up my clientele. But trust me, my prices won't always be so low, Fergie. I already got some bitches from up top, in New York, requesting me. But whoever I get right now, before my prices change, will have the same price."

"If that's the case can you do my butt, hips and breasts too?"

I never saw Charlie do breasts, but I'm sure it's the same process.

"If you come to me now, I'll do everything you want for $750."

"Oh my god, when can I come over?"

"Tomorrow. I'll hook you up real good too!"

CHAPTER EIGHTEEN

Dixie

Fergie was laying over the edge of my bed with her ass out. Although its not Charlie's work, I feel like I did a good job with the pumping. I used some of the silicone that Charlie had in her room, and I already knew what I was going to be doing for my new line of work. Sugar and Charlie better watch out, there's a new pumping queen in town!

I just finished placing Krazy Glue on the injection sites with cotton balls, when I tell her to slide back into her loose fitting sweat pants.

"I can't believe how much that shit hurts," Fergie says moving slowly. "You sure I should be lying on my ass?"

"It's up to you, but how else can I do your breasts?"

"I don't know, Dixie. Maybe I should stop right now. I already feel different with the butt shots. Like I'm moving slower or something."

"Different like what?"

"I don't know, real weak and dizzy. Do people normally feel like this after they have work done?"

"Bitch, of course! That's because you have silicone in your body. What the fuck did you think was supposed to happen? I hate when rookies get served and be talking that dumb shit. You know how many women I upgrade? About twenty a week and they all take it like a G."

"I know but—"

"Look, I'm not going to make you get nothing done you don't want too. But please recognize that my prices go up when you leave out of my front door. You my girl but this is business."

Fergie looks at me with confused eyes. I hate to put the press down on her, but without my job I needed that $750 bucks.

When she hesitates too much I say, "What you gonna do, Fergie? I got another client in an hour."

"I'll do it."

She lies on the bed face up and opens her pink velour jacket. I eye the flat male's chest she was born with, and wonder if I can really do this. Can I really give her breasts? I decide to go for what I know when after the fifteenth shot, she stopped me.

Irritated because I'm almost done I put the needle down.

"Something's wrong, Dixie," Fergie says with wide eyes. "I don't like how I feel right now. This can't be right."

I sigh. "Will you just relax already? I'm almost done. Anyway if I stop now you gonna have one titty."

"I don't care," she says breathing heavily. "I feel real light headed. I...I...I feel—"

"Just stop talking, Fergie, you're making me irritated with you right now." I stand up. "This is why I don't fuck with everybody. Had somebody else been on my table I would've been done by now."

"Maybe you should call the ambulance, Dixie," she says holding her chest. She stands up. "I don't think...I don't think I'm supposed to feel like this. I don't care what you say."

"I'm not calling no ambulance. What you gonna do is sit down there and shut the fuck up." She lies back on the bed and when I smell a strange odor, I look down at her. "Hold up, did you just shit on my bed?"

She doesn't respond. Instead she hops up and circles the room. Her eyes are wide and she looks like she is about to pass out. "Oh, my god, Dixie. I'm scared. I think I'm going to die..."

SHAY HUNTER

CHAPTER NINETEEN

Charlie

I'm driving home and trying to stop myself from crying. I just came from Sugar's house and she's so thin now, she doesn't look like the same person. She was lying in the bed, and was so frail I could see her bones. The room was crowded and I guess that's a testament to the amount of people who love her.

Although I was an emotional wreck, she was upbeat, and even made a few jokes, despite having to take air from an oxygen every few seconds. She seems to be okay with dying and I wish I could be as strong as she is, but it's so hard.

Before Sugar came into my life, I really felt like Dixie was the only person who cared about me. Even with knowing that the reason Sugar taught me the procedures, was because she wasn't going to be living, I feel like she really cares about me and my well being, and I doubt I will ever figure out why.

When we were at her house, Sugar told me and her other friends how she wanted her going away celebration to go down. She said she wanted a party, with no funeral because she didn't want people to be sad. Sugar said she wanted to be cremated, with her ashes scattered over her mother's grave, so that they can always be together. Just hearing the details, and knowing it was because she was dying, put me on edge. I remember thinking that I'm glad that her other friends were taking notes, because I was useless.

When she started dividing her assets amongst us, that's when I kindly grabbed my purse and twirled out the door. Sugar has already given me more than I could've ever asked for, and I didn't want any more. Besides, because of what she taught me, I had a large clientele, and half of the money needed for my surgery.

When my phone rings again, I quickly answer. "Hey, Luke."

"Baby girl, why you scare me like that earlier today? And why you didn't answer the phone when I called back? Do you know you had me at work about to lose my mind?"

"I'm sorry, I just left my friend's house and my mind was all over the place. I didn't tell you, but

SHAY HUNTER

she's dying and I've been an emotional wreck since I heard the news. Today was a little harder that's all."

"Oh," he exhales. "That's what it was about?"

"Yeah, and I'm sorry I called you like that. I guess I just wanted to hear your voice that's all."

"Well I almost fucked up this dude's tattoo who was on my table. You can't do me like that again, baby. You gotta come out and tell me what's going on right away so that I won't be worried sick."

"You're right and it will never happen again."

"Look, how about you come over my house tonight. Let me make you some dinner and stuff. I also know a really good massage that I was waiting to show you when the time was right. You sound stressed so what about now?"

I had been purposely avoiding going over his house. Mainly because if we were alone, with no possibility of Dixie popping up, he would want to have sex. I want to please him, I really do, and there are other things I can do to satisfy him. But I doubt sucking his dick, or letting him fuck me in the ass because I'm on my fake period, will be enough. Even though I know it will be at least six months before my surgery, I had plans to drag out our first sexual experiences as long as possible.

"Can you come over my house instead?"

"Charlie, I'm not feeling coming over your house. To tell you the truth, I was about to hurt your peoples the other day when he got fly out of his mouth with me."

"I know, but I talked to her. And she said—"

"You talked to *him*," he says. "That's your problem, Charlie. You keep treating dude like he's a lady when he's anything but. I can't stand fucking faggies, and your boy is one of them, big time."

When I pull up in front of my house I decide to round the conversation up. I'm getting frustrated with Luke and Dixon for pulling me different ways. Why do they have to argue so much?

"I'm going to call you later, and we'll make plans for the night. And try not to take everything Dixon says literally. He's always been like that."

"I don't know about all that, but you not mad at me for not feeling your boy are you?"

"No, I'm fine, I just …I just need to think Luke that's all."

"I understand, but make sure you call me and give me the verdict either which way. If you are coming over, I want to make things nice for you."

"I will."

"And Charlie…"

"Yes."

"I love you."

I'm stuck and I feel paralyzed. There are no words to describe how I feel right now. My entire life, I never had one person to tell me they loved me. Even Dixie, who would use the word loosely, never

SHAY HUNTER

came out and straight up said she loved me. And even if she did it wouldn't mean the same to me.

"Oh my god, Luke." I say parking my car in front of my house. "Are you serious?"

"You know that I am. And one day you're going to be my wife and I'm going to show you how I really feel about you."

"I don't want kids," I blurted out. I don't even know where that came from because we weren't talking about that.

He laughs. "Baby girl, the last thing I want is kids. I'm trying to build a life with you and enjoy the world, and children would hold us back. I'm selfish like that. Trust me, we good and hearing that from you, makes me know even more that I've chosen the right person."

After we say our goodbyes, and I tell him I love him three more times, I feel like I'm floating out of the car. But the moment I open the front door to my house, and see Dixie's face, I know something is going on.

"What's wrong?" I ask frantically. "You having heart pains again?" Worried, I throw my purse on the sofa.

"No, I have something to show you," he says softly.

I close the door and Dixie grabs my hand and takes me to his room. When I look down on the floor, next to the bed, I see Fergie lying on the carpet breathing shallowly.

"What's going on?" I bend down and put my hand on Fergie's arm and she moans.

"I think he's dying."

I stand up. "Dying?" I yell. "But what happened?" When I look around the room, I immediately know what happened. I see cotton balls and silicone in a cup. When I inhale deeply I can smell the odor of Krazy Glue and shit in the air. "No, no, no," I say shaking my head, "please tell me you didn't do a procedure on him. Please, Dixie."

"Yeah, we were good until I did his chest."

"But you don't even know what you doing! You haven't been trained!"

"As far as I can tell, you haven't had any formal training either. And Sugar's half dying ass don't count."

My eyes widen. How can he be so fucking stupid? In our entire relationship, I never wanted to hit him but now I'm coming dangerously close, to laying hands on him. Doesn't he realize that this could ruin me? Could ruin us? I never taught him how to do injections, so why would he think he could? Yes he followed me on a few appointments, which I knew would come back to haunt me, but I never thought it would be like this.

SHAY HUNTER

I walk over to the phone. "We have to call for the ambulance." I pick it up, but he snatches it out of my hand. "What are you doing? Fergie is still alive."

"Have you forgotten what has happened here tonight, Charlie?" he puts the phone back down.

"Yes," I yell. "You fucked up!"

"That may be true, but it won't stop the police from locking both of us up. Don't you remember," he places his hand on his chest, "what happened with Gi-Gi? It was a mistake, that's why we had to dump her body, and the same thing applies here."

"It's not the same thing," I correct him. "Gi-Gi was already dead. Fergie is alive and we can save her if we act now. I don't care what you say, Dixie, this is just wrong."

"No, what we are going to do is wait for her to die, and then bury her with Gi-Gi in the strawberry fields behind my grandma's house. Now I know you're upset but it's the only way."

I walk away from him and sit on the bed. "But this is wrong," I cry.

"And yet we still have a decision to make," he pauses. "Do we call the police, and have them arrest us? Only to investigate the crime and everything else we are into? Not to mention the fact you are out on bail. Or do we suck it up and do what we must? I mean do you really want to give everything up? Do you want to give up Luke, only to find out that he's with a real woman while you're shriveling up behind bars? Don't be stupid, Charlie."

I can't talk. I can't move. Dixie is more selfish than I ever known him to be. And I can't believe that I was living with this person, and never truly knew him. I mean I knew he could be selfish and jealous at times, but this is taking it to another level. Now it's making me think that Sugar was right. Maybe he did have something to do with Griselda's murder too. But he's also right. Why all this now? Luke said he loved me today, and I never had that before. I'm not sure I want to give it up, for something I didn't do. I'm so confused.

SHAY HUNTER

CHAPTER TWENTY

Charlie

I'm sitting on the sofa at home with Dixie drinking wine. It has been two weeks since we buried Fergie's body in the same place we buried Gi-Gi's, behind the strange house that use to belong to his grandmother. When I asked Dixie how he felt about disposing of her body that way, he said at least she wouldn't be alone since Gi-Gi was six-feet deep out there too.

Although it was becoming harder to understand Dixie, at least after we buried Fergie, he started treating me differently. It was as if something shifted inside of him. He didn't argue with Luke when he came over, and he didn't burn my phone up when I was with Sugar or hanging out late doing injections for my clients. Maybe the fact that we both held a secret, at what he called Strawberry Fields, brought us back together.

"Do you remember in the 9th grade, when that boy asked you to the prom?" Dixie asks me. "I don't know what made me think of that just now, maybe it's the liquor, but for some reason its on my mind."

"Oh my, god, yes, chile! I remember being so embarrassed." I sip the rest of the wine in my glass and top his glass off too. "He didn't care who knew he was gay in the classroom that day. He sashayed out the closet screaming, I LOVE MEN!"

Dixie laughs so hard she starts crying. "Man, I was like damn. He's just waving his flag." He wipes the tears off of his eyes. "How brave," she says shaking her head. "Bless his little faggy heart."

"The funny part is, I didn't know he was gay until that day. I think he was messing with that girl." I snap my fingers three times. "What's her name again, Dixie? I can't remember it. She wore the long black pigtails. I think she was half Indian or something. Don't you remember?"

"You talking about Natalie."

"Bitch, yes! That's her fucking name." I pause. "Dixie, she was the prettiest thing I ever seen in my life. I remember staring at her thinking, that if I died and came back to life, I wanted to be as beautiful as her."

"I was thinking the same thing," he says.

SHAY HUNTER

"Her nose, her eyes, her silky black hair," I continue recalling the features of her face in my mind. "She was just gorgeous for no reason."

"And still he chose you," Dixie smiles.

I blush although I try not too. "Yeah, something must've been wrong with him to choose me over her. But hey," I shrug, "to each, really is his own."

"Wasn't nothing wrong with that man, he knew what he wanted. Just cause a bitch got a cunt doesn't make her better. Reggie knew that shit and that's why he wanted you. The sad part is when you told him no you wouldn't go to the prom with him, he didn't come back to school for a week. From embarrassment most people thought. I still don't understand why you did that, Charlie."

I sigh. "I wasn't ready for the extra attention that going to the prom with another boy would bring. I just wanted to do me, and be done with it. Don't forget the fact that my father is a monster. He would've murdered me if I had pulled some shit like that."

"Amen to that, honey. Your father was three kinds of crazy," she sips her wine. "Anyway, I think the dude ended up marrying some boy he worked with earlier this year. You know now that the queen's can get married they are burning up the churches with marriage vows, chile."

"Ohhhh, I know them fake Christians are falling all over their knees in prayer."

Dixie shakes her head and says, "I never did get that. I mean, if I'm gay, what does that got to do with you and who you fucking? I'm not fucking you, you're not fucking me, so just live and let live." She continues waving a handkerchief for effect.

"You preaching to the choir," I admit. "Who I sleep with doesn't dictate who I am."

I shake my head. Throughout my life I have caught flack for being who I am so I feel him. Unlike Dixie, I don't flip, flop between men and women depending upon how I feel. I love me, always, while Dixie can do either or. But hey, I gotta let him live his life. At first I use to buck the system, but now I just hope for better people and better situations in my life. I stay away from straight people who don't want me around and I ask that they leave me alone too.

"You ever talk to Sherry again? Because I still can't believe what she did to you at that party. By telling Bernard you fucked him."

"Girl, you know she tried to say she didn't tell him when I ran into her. She came up to me one day when I was leaving your house, I think I was going to work. Anyway, at first I wasn't going to stop but I had to know why she was so foul. She cried to me and told me she didn't say anything to Bernard and that she didn't know who did. I don't trust that bitch though."

"That bitch said something to him," Dixie says pointing at me. "Don't believe the hype. I was there, and I know she told him you fucked dude. Why else would he bash your face in like that?"

Even though it was the past, it still hurt my feelings. I loved Sherry, and I still love her now, and I could never imagine why she would hurt me like that. She knew horror stories about faggies I knew, who were beat to a pulp when their secret came out.

When my cell phone rings I answer it. Dixie jumps up and says, "You take your call, boo, I'm 'bout to cook the spaghetti."

"Thanks, Dixie," I say. I focus on my call. "Hey, Luke, what you doing?"

"Thinking about you. I just finished tattooing this nigga's arm. He got a full length body tat of his girl, and I'm thinking his bitch was beautiful, but she still can't hold a candle to mine."

"Why do you do me like that? Getting me all excited and shit, when you talk to me like I'm the one."

"Cause I love you, Charlie. You know that. Sometimes I think the way I'm feeling is crazy, because I wasn't that type of dude before I met you. Love wasn't my thing. You know? I was the kinda nigga who vowed to always be single, but you changed that."

It feels like butterflies are fluttering through my stomach and I'm smiling so high my cheekbones ache. "You always know what to say to me, Luke."

"I just say what's on my mind." He pauses. "I'm just glad you like it. But look, I wanna talk to you about something real quick."

My heart rate increases. Although things have been going great between us, and he told me he loves me, it's always in the back of my mind that he'll find out that I'm not a woman and dump me.

"Sure, baby, what's up?"

"I been thinking a lot about our situation, and I want to go a little further. So, I want you to meet my parents."

The room is spinning and I pull my knees near my chest because I can't take it. "What...I mean...why?"

"Why?" he chuckles. "I want you to meet them because you're my lady. And you know what, I never brought anybody home so it's going to be major for them too. But I don't care because I want them to see who I love."

"But what if they don't like me?"

"Then I won't fuck with them. I'm done with the weak shit, Charlie. They are going to either have to accept who I want in my life, or they can stay out of it. The choice is theirs but I know my family will love you, especially my mother."

"This will mean a lot to you won't it?"

"It will mean everything to me. *Everything.*"

"Then I'll do it."

"That's my, wifey. Look, another client just walked in. And more than likely I'll be here all night because he's starting a sleeve. I'll call you back with the plan later okay?"

"Okay, daddy."

"I love it when you call me that."

When he gets off of the phone I walk into the kitchen to tell my girl the good news.

Before I can even say anything he's grinning. "Aw shit...what juicy secrets has Luke whispered in your ear this time? Do tell."

"He wants me to meet his parents."

The smile is wiped off of his face and is replaced with an expression that resembles the look of jealously. "What the fuck do you mean meet his parents?" he stirs the ground turkey meat in the pan.

"That's what he said," I say softly. "He wants his parents to know who I am. You should've heard him, Dixie, he was all excited and shit."

"And for obvious reasons you not going right?" he turns on the eye under the spaghetti.

"Actually I am, Dixie. He says it's important to him so I have no choice."

"So what you gonna do when you get there, show them your dick? Because let us not forget that you aren't a woman." He turns the eye off of the meat. "Which is who he thinks he's introducing his family too. If you go you'll be making a big mistake."

"Dixie, we already talked about what will happen if things don't end well. Luke says if they have a problem with me, then he'll cut them off."

"And you think that shit is cool?" he pops the top to the spaghetti sauce and pours it into the meat. "For someone to cut off their parents just for you? What kind of person are you?"

"Dixie, why are you acting like this?"

"You know what, at first I was afraid you were going to get hurt, but now I'm thinking Luke's the one who needs protection. You don't deserve him, because it's obvious that the boy is way in love with you, and you not being honest."

"Dixie, why are you talking like this? Me and Luke's thing doesn't have anything to do with you."

"It will when you have to cry in my ear, after he finds out you's a boy."

"Are you saying you gonna tell him?"

He turns the eye off on the spaghetti and walks away.

CHAPTER TWENTY-ONE

Dixie

You know I really tried to start all over with Charlie, and make things right, but now I get the impression that she thinks she's better than me. I got something for that ass though, and she won't see this move coming.

I'm in the bathroom at home throwing bundles of toilet paper in the toilet to stop it up. Then when I get to the brown carton roll in the center, I wet it with water and watch it expand. Then I throw it in the toilet along with some yellow lemonade. The brownness of the carton, and the yellow water, makes it look like I pissed and shit. After my scene was set up, I disconnected the latch in the toilet so that it won't flush.

After I'm done I walk into the hallway and then into Charlie's room. He's on the phone, probably talking to Luke again. "Charlie, the toilet is not flushing so I'll need you to wait on the plumber. I called him already so he should be on his way."

She looks back at me, sits the phone down and says, "Do you know what time they getting here? Because I have an appointment in two hours with a client."

"No, but either way I can't stay. As you know I have an appointment tonight with this girl who wants me to help run her beauty salon. I won't be out too long, so I'll hurry back."

"I guess I don't have a choice."

"You don't if you want to live here," I say rolling my eyes.

With Charlie out of the way, I waltz out of his room and the house. Feeling confident I jump into my truck and make it to my destination in thirty minutes. Surprisingly the tattoo parlor is empty when I get there. And Luke is standing at a drawing table with his back faced my direction.

I thought about something last night. Luke fights with me on a daily basis. It reminds me of when I was a kid, and how I use to pick on the girls or boys I thought was cute. I was only mean to the ones I liked. And maybe, just maybe, Luke was mean to me, and asked Charlie to meet his parents to get me to come to him. Think about it, we haven't fought in awhile, and now he says something to Charlie that I'm certain he knew would set me off.

When the doorbell rings, indicating that someone had walked in Luke says, "I'll be right with you." He doesn't bother to look up at me.

"Take your time," I say in a low voice.

Maybe it's the melody in my voice, because this time he turns around and looks at me. He throws down the pencil and angrily stomps in my direction. "What the fuck are you doing here, Dixon?" He's so close, and breathing so hard, that his warm breath brushes against my cheek.

"I didn't come here to argue with you, Luke." I walk around him and look at a few tattoos on his wall. "So relax, because I do come in peace."

"If you didn't come to argue, then what did you come here for? Because it ain't nothing about you I like." He walks up behind me, and his manliness turns me on.

"I came here to let you know that Charlie is not being forthcoming with you." I turn around and look into his eyes. "And I know we have our problems, you and I that is, but I don't want to see you get your feelings hurt."

"My feelings hurt?" he places his hands over his chest. "You trying to say Charlie wants what we have to be over?"

The disappointment I hear in his voice causes my stomach to swirl. Ms. Charlie really did well this time because she got this nigga roped.

"I'm saying she's lying to you about who she is. Charlie has a history of this type of behavior, and it's high time that you know."

"And what type of behavior do you exhibit? Because if Charlie told you something in confidence and you are here to tell me, in my opinion it's kind of foul. Real friends don't do that type shit."

"You always think you know everything about me don't you, Luke?"

"Until I see a change, it will always be how I feel when it comes to you."

I walk up to the drawing table by the window. When I glance out of the window, I see my truck next to his black Infiniti. I look down at his work. It's a picture of a woman holding a child.

"You did this really well. Did Charlie tell you she can't have kids?"

He laughs. "Look, I got some work to do and it's obvious you here to play games. With that said, I'm not entertaining you no more. So I need you to turn out the same door you just came in."

"Luke, what can I do to help our relationship grow?"

"You can leave me and my girl alone and let us do us."

SHAY HUNTER

I'm just about to bounce on him when I see something that changes everything through the window. Slowly I unlatch the buckle to my pants, and then I unzipped my tight jeans. Within the time you can bat an eye, I push them down to my ankles and bend over.

"What the fuck are you doing?" Luke yells. "Pull you fucking pants up, nigga!"

"Relax, Luke, I'm just giving you some of this good boy band pussy because I know you want it so badly. Don't fake on me, Luke. The world is yours right now. Take it."

He runs up behind me and grabs me roughly. "I want you out of here! Now!" he yelled while grabbing me around my waste, and wrestling with me, in an attempt to get me away from his table.

"Come on, Luke." I wiggle my ass. "Don't fake. Come get these goodies."

"Nigga, I will kill you. I don't fuck with raunchy ass faggies like you."

"Try it once, big boy. I know you'll like it."

When I glance at the window, and see the reflection of the person I was waiting on come through the door I yell, "Rape! Rape! Get off of me, Luke!"

"Fuck is you talking 'bout, ain't nobody raping you!"

From the window's position I know exactly what it looks like. My jeans are on the floor and Luke is behind me, playing rough. I could not have asked for a better situation if I tried. Instead of telling him that Charlie's a man, and making Charlie angry with me, I decide to get rid of Luke all together. It's for the best anyway. He would have only broken Charlie's heart, or got his feelings hurt once he discovered that his sweetheart has a dick.

"What's going on in here?" Charlie says in a shivering voice.

"Baby, uh, what are you doing here?" Luke asks. "I thought you said you had to wait on the plumber? I was on my way to your house after I finished my last drawing."

"I fixed the toilet myself," she says looking at me as I pull up my clothes. "Can somebody tell me what's going on please?"

I step up to her. "Charlie, Luke called me over here on the way to the salon. He said he wanted to talk to me about—"

"Bitch, why you lying," Luke roared. "I never told you I wanted to meet you. I was doing my work and you showed up on that dumb shit. Now tell her the truth before I—"

"Before you do what, nigga?" I ask stepping to his face.

Luke got me fucked up. I might be dressed in woman's clothing, but I'm nowhere near a punk. I know how to handle mine and if he tries me just like everybody else, he'll find out. As fucked up as this may be, I'm really doing it for Charlie. She needs me to do this so that I can get him out of her life before she gets hurt. Just like she needed me to call her boss Frieda and tell her that she was stealing from the register. I got tired of Charlie coming home every night complaining about how tired she was. I wanted to take care of her, because I love her. I know she doesn't want to be with me, but soon she'll find out that I'm the only one she needs.

Luke goes around me and walks up to Charlie. He places a hand on each side of her face. "Baby, I love you, do not let this faggy come between us. We onto something real now, Charlie. You got me wanting to change my life for you. Please, I'm begging you, move out and move in with me. I can make you so happy if you let me."

I walk towards the door. "Charlie, are you coming with me or not?"

"Don't go with him, baby," Luke says crying. "Don't leave me, because he's lying and all he wants to do is hurt you."

"Charlie," I yell clapping my hands. She immediately looks at me and I hold her attention. "It's time to go. Now I know you love him, but this nigga is foul! So the question is, are you coming with me or not? Because after this, you won't get another chance."

CHAPTER TWENTY-TWO

Charlie

It's been weeks since I've seen Luke and I miss him terribly. He calls me almost everyday, and a part of me is relieved because it makes me think maybe he does love me, even though he did me so foul. And what about what he tried to do with my friend?

If there is one thing I know, its that men who have hatred toward gay men, like Luke has toward faggies, are more than likely hiding something inside. And in this instance it's the fact that he was attracted to Dixie the entire time. I know this is twisted, but I don't want to be with a man who wants another man. I want a man who loves me for who I am inside, and who I want to be. A woman.

I'm sitting on the sofa drinking my third glass of wine, trying to get my mind together. I had five

SHAY HUNTER

appointments earlier and I'm beat. I had one girl who had a botched ass job who I had to pad with more silicone to make it look better. I also had a face to do, because this queen wanted extra cheeks, even though she had enough. I had a lady who wanted her hips done and two people who wanted injections in their thighs. I'm exhausted. But even though I'm irritated, I know I'm only ten thousand dollars away from getting the money needed for my surgery. So if you ask me if it's worth it, I must say hell yes.

When I turn on the radio to let the music fill my soul, Dixie switches into the house wearing an ugly red curly wig, a red sequined dress and a smile. Where the fuck did she just come from a *Tootsie* movie convention? She looked wretched.

"I know what I want for my birthday next month," she sings to me.

"What?" I say dryly, sipping more wine.

"Wow, you don't sound too happy. When it's your birthday I always try to make sure things are good for you. You'd think you'd put a little more effort into my birthday, especially if I say I have a birthday wish, since I normally never do. But I guess that's too much to ask."

"Why do you gotta always do that?" I sigh.

"Do what?"

"Throw it in my face whenever you do something for me? I'm getting tired of that shit, Dixie. As a matter of fact, don't do nothing else for me if you gonna throw it in my face every time. I'm good on your favors."

Her eyes widen and she looks at my glass and the bottle of wine on the floor. "Is that the vino talking?"

"You not even trying to listen to me. "

"I am listening, Charlie. It's just that you never talked to me like that before. Its like you got an attitude with me or something."

"And I'm allowed to have an attitude," I sip all of the wine and put the glass down on the table. "I don't have to be happy all the time. I don't have to wear a smile on my face just because you ask me. I'm okay with being me."

She sits her purse down. "I think you better watch who you talking too."

I don't know what came over me, but suddenly I laugh hysterically. For the past five years I have allowed her and my father to dictate how I think, act and feel. I'm tired of it. And I don't know if the feeling will wear off tomorrow after I have had time to think about it, but for now, I don't care.

"I'm talking to you, Dixon Wood. A human being and another queen just like me."

"You must be drunk, because you're talking crazy."

"If that's what you feel, so be it. But please understand that I know exactly what I'm saying."

SHAY HUNTER

"You know what, I'm not going to even let you ruin my vibe." she smiles.

"Oh, goody, goody, goody," I say sarcastically clapping my hands together.

"Anyway, as you know my birthday is coming up, and I decided that I want some work."

"Work on..."

"My butt, face and cheeks.

I look at his red freckled face. "Dixie, I'm not doing you, so if you looking at me to do the work, forget about it."

"Why not? If it's about the money I got your little coins, sweetheart. It's not a problem, Ms. Charlie."

"It's not about the money. I'm not doing you because I don't want too. If you want injections done, get 'em by somebody else."

"But you the best. Sugar taught you everything she knew."

"And here in lies the problem."

"Why don't you want to do me," he frowns. "Is it because you afraid of a little competition around here?"

"The real question needs to be why do you want them? Dixie, I have been living with you for years. I've watched you dress like a woman on Tuesdays, Fridays and Monday, and then like a confused butch queen on the other days, when you go out the door to fuck some dumb girl. I'm not adding to the confusion so the answer is no."

"You are so fucking jealous," he says.

I look at the mess that is his face and bust out into laughter. "Never that, sweetheart. You asked me to pump you, and I said no. When you think about it there's really not a whole lot to it. I'm entitled to say no."

"You mad at me that the secret came out about Luke aren't you?"

"There you go again, mixing the truths. One thing has nothing to do with the other, Dixie. I said no, so it will be no, just drop the shit already."

"You are going to do me and you will do your best work too," he says, "this I know."

"And if I don't?"

"I will let the needles that I buried with Fergie and Gi-Gi stay in their graves forever. Depending upon how I feel, I might even put a call into the police. Keep in mind your fingerprints are on both needles, because I wore gloves when I did Fergie's injections."

My body trembles. "Why would you do something like that? What would possess you to bury evidence?"

"Because I'm so tired of not being able to trust you. And just so you know, I was going to take them back out after I determined that you were loyal. But now...well now I don't know what to do."

SHAY HUNTER

"You really are a snake aren't you?"

She stands up and walks toward the kitchen. "If that's what you gotta call me, to feel better about you, I'll be that and then some. It's quite alright."

I walk over to her. "You hate me don't you?"

She laughs. "Why would I hate you, Charlie? You serve your purpose?"

"And what purpose is that?"

"You allow me to realize that I am capable of mercy and grace. I mean think about it for a minute, Charlie. If I wasn't in your life where would you have been? I saved you."

"Probably happy?"

"Oh yeah? With who? Your father?" She laughs. "Bitch, the moment he saw your gay hand sloop downward, he wanted nothing to do with you. What about all the times he told you to sit out in the car, when he had business to handle because he didn't want his friends to see you? Huh? You were a disgrace, and I gave you life, honey. You should be kissing my feet."

"You know the saddest part about all of this," I cry.

"No, what is it, moon shine?"

"The sad part is I love you," Dixie. "Yes I was in need of help, but there were many people who told me to stay clear of you. And I ignored all of them because I love you, and look where it got me. Stabbed in the face."

"No, no, sweetheart. You're telling the tale all wrong, it got you in the company of a star." She pauses. "I don't see a problem. Do you?"

I'm so over her right now. When I walk back into the living room I can see my phone vibrating. When I glance at the screen I see Sugar is calling me. I answer the phone and say, "Hey, Sugar, how you feel?"

"I need you to come over now. It's very important."

SHAY HUNTER

CHAPTER TWENTY-THREE

Charlie

I'm sitting on the edge of the bed staring at my dear friend Sugar. I'm at his house. Although I know his reason for being ill, I can't get past the transformation. He doesn't look anything like he did the first time I started doing business with him. He has lesions everywhere, and he resembles a corpse.

"The doctor says my CD4 count is under 50," he tells me. "I have to stay on bed rest to avoid infections. At first I was trying to do more, say goodbye to my friends and make a few visits, but now I think I'm going to start paying attention to him."

"Have you been taking your medicine? Like we agreed upon, Sugar?"

"I honestly did but now it's too late. All I can do is relax and take it easy in my last days." I wipe the tears away. "Please, Charlie, try not to cry when you look at me. I want to see a smile on that beautiful face so that I'm in a good mood." He rubs my hand. "But I'm calling you here because I'm leaving you something."

I sigh. "Sugar, I don't want anything from you, and I told you that already."

"This ain't about you," he responds in a weak voice. "It's about me and what I want to do for you. And if you love me you'll allow me too."

"You've done enough already. It's because of you that I have almost enough money to get my surgery. I don't want anything but for you to get better. Can you give me that? If not I'm good."

He smiles. "You are such a brat, when you want to be. But you're also adorable."

I smile and blow a kiss. "Well I do try."

When my cell phone goes off I notice its Luke. To this day, even though we weren't together, my heart skips a beat whenever I see his number. "Is that your sweetie again?" Sugar asks.

"He *was* my sweetie," I sigh, throwing my cell phone down. "And stop playing games because I know I told you that already. I'm done with Luke, I can't deal with that type of pain anymore."

"I can't believe that you are actually allowing Dixie's moose face ass to come in between you and that fine ass man of yours. Sweetie, are you sure you not the one who's dying?"

SHAY HUNTER

"He tried to rape her, Sugar. You weren't there. I saw the whole thing."

"I don't know what you saw but it wasn't no Luke raping Dixie's red ass. And you don't believe that either. You were just looking for an out, and that performance that snake put on gave you a way to back out."

"What are you talking about, Sugar? I love Luke!"

"I know you do, which is why you shouldn't let a fraud steal him away from you. It's a shame. What you need to do is face the fact that you need to speak to him honestly about your situation."

"But he doesn't know who I am."

"You mean that you're a beautiful woman who resides in a man's body? Listen, baby, since you are planning to throw him away anyway, you might as well tell him. I got a feeling that he'll give you the benefit of the doubt if you give him a chance. But by all means please don't get rid of your man."

"It's hard, Sugar." I shake my head. "You making shit sound easy but it's not that simple. Niggas, don't like to be with women who they find out are men."

"You the one making shit hard, Charlie. As you know I'm dying. But a funny thing happens when you are this close to death," he pauses, "you realize that the things that you worried about, or the things that held you in fear for so long, were never as bad as you thought."

"I don't know what to do," I say. "I feel exhausted.

"Just give him a chance, Charlie. Please."

I shake my head and decide to keep shit all the way real with Sugar. "There's something else I need to share with you."

"Go ahead," he says. "You know I'm here for you."

"I accidently killed Gi-Gi, after a procedure. She got MRSA and—"

"But that wasn't your fault."

"I know, but shortly after that, Dixie killed Fergie by accident when he tried to mimic me and pump her. We buried both of them at his grandmother's house, well behind her house. A few hundred feet from a strawberry field."

"So if you killed someone and he did, that should make you two even."

"At first I thought it did, but yesterday he blackmailed me into doing injections for him and I don't want to."

"Mercy," he says. "You have a heavy situation on your plate." He takes in oxygen. "Why didn't you tell me before?"

"I was embarrassed and didn't want to disappoint you. But for as long as you live, I will never allow that to happen again." I pause. "Outside of the blackmailing, whenever me and Dixie get into it, he complains of chest pains due to his heart murmur. And if something happens to him if I leave, I'm afraid that will be my fault too, and I'll never be able to live with myself."

"Charlie, you are taking too much on, baby. Way too much. Now I heard that Gi-Gi and Fergie were missing, and the sad part about it is that the damage is done. Don't say anything to anybody else about that. Repeat it to no one. As a matter of fact, whenever Dixie brings it up act like you don't know what he's talking about."

"Okay," I say. "You think that's going to be enough?"

"Everything will work out in time. Trust me."

CHAPTER TWENTY-FOUR

Sugar

"Sugar, I know you care about this queen, for whatever reason, but the last thing on your mind should be Charlie and her problems," Monique says to her sickly friend as she stares down at her while she lies in the bed. "She's a big girl. She can handle her own life."

"I know she can handle her own, but I want to give her some assistance along the way. Now I've given you all your instructions," she continues looking at her two friends, who were both dressed fabulously in drag. "And I need them carried out as part of my last wish."

"We got the plan," Courtney says. "Can you tell us why?"

SHAY HUNTER

Sugar pulls a puff of oxygen and says, "If I tell you, will it make the job easier?"

"Yes."

"A year ago at this party I did something I can't take back."

"More info, darling," Monique says. "We *are* queens. You know we are nothing without our stories."

"Well some time back I found out that Bernard was fucking with this Twinkie in high school. I found out when I went through his phone, back when I was on my psycho shit, and I got exactly what I was looking for. My feelings hurt."

"You mean *THE* Bernard?" Monique inquires. "The one who broke your heart and later gave you AIDS?"

"Yes, the one and only," he continues. "Well anyway, when we first moved in together, I use to follow him all the time. I didn't catch him doing anything for a while, until three months after we were together. I followed him and caught him fucking this teenager after coming out of the gym. I was devastated by this shit, girls. You know Bernard was my everything. And ya'll know I did all I could for that nigga."

"That's fucked up, because I really liked him at one point," Monique adds. "I remember when you bought his first car and some more shit. "

"It happens to the best girls," she sighs. "But anyway, I never said anything to him about what I saw. I just waited until I found out about this party he was going too. Something told me he was going to see the teenager he had relations with. And as sure as my name is Kenny Sugar, I saw the cute little Twinkie he fucked at the gym walk into the party with some chick."

"Oh my, goodness. What did you do?" Monique asks grabbing at her chest.

"I paid my cousin Mirando, to spread the rumor that Bernard was fucking niggas at the party. Because you know he wanted to keep his lifestyle on the low. I was so mad, that I also told Mirando to tell people that the Twinkie said it."

They both gasped.

"Wait a minute," Denise says covering her mouth. "The Twinkie was Charlie?"

"Yes, and I never forgave myself for what he did to him, and his face. I knew it would be bad, but never thought it would be like that. So last year, when Bernard died from AIDS, I felt like I had to do something about it."

"So you took him under your wing?"

"Yes, and now he needs my help." Sugar looks up at them. "This is where you girls come in. Is that enough reason for you to help me now?"

"Say no more," Denise says springing into action. "The queens are on the job!"

SHAY HUNTER

"My girls!"

CHAPTER TWENTY-FIVE

Dixie

I'm lying face up on Charlie's table, in our house, getting my face done. I wanted him to make my cheeks a little fuller, so that I can have the feminine features women are known for. I know Charlie doesn't respect my decision to transition over to a woman, but he'll have to deal with it. He's not the only person who wants to be beautiful around here anymore.

When I see a tear crawling down his face as he pushes the needle into my skin, I sigh. "What are you thinking about now, Charlie? Because you should be focusing on my face."

He wipes his tears away and looks into my eyes, while the needle enters my cheek. The pain is

SHAY HUNTER

riveting and I don't see how some queens do it on the regular.

"I'm sorry, my mind wandered I guess."

"Well does your mind wander every time you doing work? Because I'm starting to take this shit personal." I focus on the light above my head. "I am a paying customer you know."

"Just what are you paying me again?" Charlie asks. "Because I'm confused. As far as I know you're getting this work done for free."

"Of course I'm paying you," I say. "For this work I have agreed to remove the needles from the corpses hands, that contain your fingerprints under the ground."

"You can be really evil."

I laugh. "Everybody knows I'm a mothafucking monster."

Her lips twitch. "What are you going to do when this is all done, and you realize you can't slip into your jeans anymore when you want to play butch? What are you going to do when you can't wear your baseball caps to the back, and pull up on unsuspecting women when you want to see if you still got it?"

I have thought about that. And yes it is true that every now and again, I do enjoy some good pussy. But I believe my game is so perfect, that even with perky cheeks I can get anybody to do anything I want.

Unlike Charlie, I'm not weak. I'm not scared to try two things that are polar opposites from the other. I like pussy every now and again, and I enjoy getting fucked and getting my dick sucked too. If you ask me Charlie is just jealous because I can be all things.

"You putting a little silicone in my cheeks won't stop—"

"Oh my, God," Charlie screams. When he removes the syringe he doesn't have a needle attached.

My eyes widen and I pop up from the massage table. "What did you do, Charlie?" I touch my face and my finger is pricked by something. When I lower my hand, I see a trickle of red blood.

"What the fuck have you done, bitch?"

"Dixie, I'm so sorry," she says backing up. "I...the needle. It...it popped off into your face."

"What the fuck do you mean it popped off into your face?" I jump up and approach her. "What did you do to me?"

"Dixie, I don't know what happened. I—"

"I'll tell you what happened, you too busy thinking about Luke's bum ass. If you would've focus on what the fuck you were doing, instead of thinking of a nigga who doesn't want you anymore, this would never have happened." I walk to the bathroom and I can hear her feet slapping against the hardwood floors behind me.

"I do have a lot on my mind, that's why I didn't want to do it, but it was a mistake. Dixie, please forgive me. I'm so sorry. I really am."

When I make it to the bathroom, I move inside slowly. I want to see what he has done, but I don't want to face the mirror. The moment I see my face, I stumble backwards. There's a huge lump sitting under my eye. I remove the needle, and blood pours down my face.

Looking at her I say, "Charlie, what, what happened?"

"The silicone moved. I never had it happen before."

"Well fix it," I yell. "Get it out of my face!"

"Dixie," she says softly. "I'm not a doctor, I don't know how to do that shit."

"I know that, bitch! If you were a doctor this would not have happened."

"Hear me out," she says, "I'm not a doctor, so there is no way I can take it out without tearing into your face. And I don't want to do that because I don't want to make things worse."

"So let me get this straight," I ball up my hands. "You're telling me that I'm stuck like this for the rest of my life? Is that what you're saying?"

"I'm saying that I can't fix your face, Dixie, I'm so sorry."

"You did this shit on purpose didn't you? You were mad at me, and you didn't want to be the only person looking pretty around here."

Her eyes widen. "What? No," she shakes her head. "I wasn't even thinking about no shit like that. It was an accident, Dixie."

"Yeah right, the moment you found out that Luke was interested in me, you have had it in for me. Just come out and tell the truth, Charlie."

"You are so far off right now it's ridiculous."

I step up to her. "You are going to take this shit out of my face or I'm going into the hospital. And when I do, I'm going to tell them that you put this shit into my face. And you know what's going to happen?"

She doesn't talk.

"You going to get locked up."

"You know what, I'm so sick of this blackmailing shit," she throws her hands up in the air. "At this point you can do whatever it is you want. I can't deal with this shit no more, Dixie. If you feel like that's the best decision for you there's nothing I can do to change it, and I'm not going to try anymore."

"I think you believe I'm fucking around. But I'm not. I'm so serious right now."

"I believe you, Dixon. And I also know that I'm tired of fighting with you. Yes I fucked up your face, but it was by accident."

SHAY HUNTER

"If you think I believe that, then that's on you." She walks away and leaves me in the bathroom.

When she's gone I look at my altered face. One cheek is bigger than the other, and blood is crawling down it. Under my eye is a big lump and when I push it down, it pops back up.

I don't know what I'm going to do yet. But I do know this, she will pay for what she has done to me.

CHAPTER TWENTY-SIX

Charlie

I'm in my car trying not to hyperventilate. As the days go by, I swear I'm starting to hate Dixie. I know she thinks I meant to poke her on purpose, but that was so far from the truth.

Before doing her face, which she made me do, I was told by a queen down club Wiggles that they saw Luke with a beautiful woman. Since we broke up, and they don't know about it yet, I tried to play it off like I knew about the date. They said that they were laughing it up at a restaurant in Washington DC. I kept imagining this real woman, who was prettier than me, thinner than me and able to give him everything he wanted. The thought alone tore me up inside, and I forgot what I was doing when I was working on Dixie. I don't even remember her talking to me, until she started screaming.

As angry as Dixie makes me, I would never intentionally hurt her, and I know she doesn't believe me.

When my phone rings, I pick it up. It's Belize from club Wiggles, who is also a good friend of mine. "Belize, can I call you back? I got a lot of shit on my mind right now."

"Oh my, goodness, are you okay, honey? You sound terrible!"

"Not really," I respond pulling out of my parking lot, going god knows where. "It's been a long and trying day. But after some time, I'll be okay."

"This doesn't have anything to do with Dixie's ass now does it? Because I been told you that you need to get rid of that butch queen. She's a downer."

"Actually it's partially to do with her, but to tell you the truth its a little bit of everything."

"Well I hate to add to your burdens, but whatever happened between you and her has been broadcast all over Wiggles."

"What do you mean?" My heart is rocking inside of my chest.

"Chile, she done called down to Wiggles and told everybody that you poked her in the face with needles, and messed it up while she was sleep. She telling people that she looks like a rock monster and everything. I mean what happened over there?"

My mouth hangs open. "Are you serious?"

"Girl, yes, and it's terrible. She's asking for coins to get her face fixed and everything. But not one queen even bothered to grab their wig to flip it over, honey. She's done."

I pull over and park my car. For a moment I don't speak, just stare out into the world. What's happening to me? I don't know who I am anymore. I feel done for. Confused and sad.

"Charlie, baby, are you there?"

"Yes," I say wiping more tears. "I'm here, Belize. I'm sorry, but like I said earlier it's been a bad day."

"Do you still pray? I remember you use to be the first one at the bedside of our queens who needed the word when they were sick. That's why people come to your rescue when you need them. That's why, not one person placed a coin in the wig to get Dixie's face fixed. She's a bad person but you're different. So I gotta repeat the question again, do you still pray? Or are you over there letting Dixie change you for the worst?"

I think about what she says. Although prayer had been a part of my life in the past, lately I haven't had a chance to do it. I'm filled with hate and revenge all of the time, and I desperately want the feelings to go away. I don't know what kind of person it will make me, but I do know that I'm tired of being a push over. I'm tired of being the one that people always take advantage of.

Instead of answering her question I say, "I have to go, Belize. I really am sorry." I hang up.

I don't feel like praying right now. I feel like giving a certain person exactly what she deserves, and that's exactly what I'm going to do.

CHAPTER TWENTY-SEVEN

Charlie

Yesterday was a rough day for me, with what happened to Dixie and all. But today was a new day. I had a plan and I wasn't going to let anyone get in the way of it.

With my strategy in mind, as I strutted into Sugar's bedroom, and saw Courtney and Monique, two of Sugar's major friends, I knew something was wrong. I place my purse on the table and say, "What's going on?" I walk over to the bed and placed my hand on Sugar's foot, which is covered under the sheet.

"Tell her, Courtney," Sugar says to her. "She needs to know."

Courtney walks up to me. "First I want to tell you that I'm a Candy Striper at the hospital, so I'm giving you straight fact. I work there when I can, mainly on the weekends. Well today I spoke to one of the nurses and found out something about your friend Dixie that you may not like."

"Like what?" I ask, with my heart dancing inside of my chest.

"For starters he doesn't have a heart murmur."

"What are you talking about? Of course he has a heart murmur. When I use to stay at his house, with his family, he took medicine almost every day. I don't know where you got your information from but it's wrong."

"Did you ever see his parents give him medicine?" Sugar asks, before breathing within her oxygen mask.

I think about all of the times as a teenager he took medicine. He would take something in an orange bottle, when he came home from school, and when we got into an argument. He would always get his way because I would feel so guilty about upsetting him, which caused him pain that I would do whatever he asked. But throughout his life, I never saw his mother give him anything.

"I don't think that she did give him anything."

"That's because he's lying," Courtney continues. "As a matter of fact, the doctor's won't even allow him to register at the hospital anymore, unless he has the approval of a psychologist. The last time he came in for some help with his fake condition, they tried to commit him into an institution but he ran. That girl is off. All the way off."

I'm so perplexed that I sit down in a chair. "I'm confused." I run my hand over my face. "You mean all of these years, that he has been getting me to do things because of his heart murmur, he doesn't even have one?"

"The boy is as healthy as a teenager, and here's the thing, I don't know what's going on, but apparently he hates you, and tells everyone he comes in contact with how ungrateful you are," Monique adds.

"I told you that I asked for you for months, but he would never give you my message," Sugar says. "He's a hater." He places the mask on his face.

"You need to get away from him, honey," Courtney says. "If you don't, I fear he will be the death of you."

Sugar removes his mask. "You hear what we're saying, Charlie? This man needs to be far away from you. Far, far away."

"I know I have to leave, but there is something I have to do first." I'm so angry I can murder Dixie. This mothafucka has taken a chunk of my life behind a bunch of lies. I can't believe I let him play me like this.

"What do you have to do," Sugar asks. "If you're worried about the bodies, we took care of that too."

SHAY HUNTER

I look at him with wide eyes. "What, what do you mean?" I observe Courtney and Monique who seem as cool as fans. "Both Fergie and Gi-Gi?" I was afraid to mention their names since Sugar told me not too. But I figure based on how they're acting, they must know already.

"We got the bodies up and out, honey," Courtney says. "You lucky Sugar loves you so much, because it was a lot of work for us two girls. Now that she has a spot for you in her heart, we do too. And there is one thing we don't do is leave our babies hanging."

"But how did you know where they were?"

"That's another weird part about Dixie," Courtney says. "He spends a lot of time at that old house talking to the ground, and we followed him one day. I wouldn't be surprised if he has some more people buried out there. We only dug up the two fresh graves though."

"Yeah, we think his mama could be there," Monique says. "Nobody has been able to find her in years. Who knows where she is."

His mother has been gone for years, and he hates talking about her. The room feels like it's spinning. I was in the company of a monster all this time, and I'm afraid that he might hurt somebody else. I have to do something.

"She's heard enough, girls," Sugar says. "Give me a few moments alone with her."

They both kiss him on the cheek and then walk out of the room. He pats the bed beside him and I take a seat. "I don't want you letting that monster change you, Charlie, and I realize this is a lot to handle. But please listen to me, you are not him."

"He'll never change me," I say, although thoughts of hurting him play in my mind.

"Then why do your eyes show me something differently?"

"Maybe you're looking at them the wrong way."

"Charlie, please listen to me, DO…NOT…LET…HIM…CHANGE…YOU," he says slowly. "You're a great person and you are destined. And you finally got enough money to have the surgery that you always desired. Find out who you want to be now, your dream job, and then stop the injections. You understand what I'm saying? It's time to move on."

"I know, Sugar," I say softly.

"Good, now I got something else for you."

She picks up the cell phone on the bed, dials a number and looks at the door. I follow her gaze.

SHAY HUNTER

CHAPTER TWENTY-EIGHT

Charlie

Luke and I are sitting in the living room inside of Sugar's house. He's staring at me, and my heart is beating so rapidly I can hear it pulsating inside of my ear. He just had a haircut, and I can smell the scent of soap and expensive cologne mixing on his skin. The only thing I want to do right now is kiss him, and make love.

"Before you say anything let me speak," Luke says touching my leg. "I know what you saw when Dixie came to my shop the other day, looked really bad from your view point. And I get how you could've thought one thing, even though it was another. But, baby, you have to listen, I never, ever wanted that nigga a day in my life. Never."

"I know."

"Don't tell me you know if you don't," he says placing both of my hands into his. "Don't make me think you're feeling me on this if you're not."

"I believe you, baby," I say, before breathing in his scent again.

"Then why didn't you come back to me? Why you leave me out there in the world like that alone? When you know I wanted nothing more than to be with you? Tell me, baby because right now I don't understand."

"Because I used it to hide another secret," I look down at my hands that I took from his and place in my lap. "That I didn't want you to know, because I was afraid you would leave me."

"What would make me leave you? Who could separate me from you that I wouldn't murder? Do you know I wanted to lay hands on Dixon when he did that shit back at my shop? I'm the kind of person who always moves on how I feel, and I could've killed him with my bare hands."

I think back to when I remembered where I knew him from, it was from the night I was locked up. He was brought into the cell right before I was released. He was locked up apparently for fighting, so I know he's telling the truth.

"I stopped myself from doing that because I love you so much. Because I knew if I hurt him, that it would separate me from you forever, Charlie, and I didn't want to risk that. Do you know I never prayed for anything or anyone in my entire life, but I prayed for you. I been praying ever since you left me that day, and today I got a call from Sugar telling me to come over. Now that man back there, is a real friend, and you are lucky to have him."

He gives me chills. "If that is true, why were you with another woman the other day? Having lunch?"

"When?" he asks with wide eyes.

"Some days ago."

He laughs but I don't think anything is funny. "Are you going to answer the question or what?"

"Baby, I don't mean to laugh, but this shit is comical," he chuckles. "Was the woman extremely beautiful?"

"That's what I heard." I grit my teeth.

"Baby, that beautiful woman was my mother. People tell her all the time that she looks like my sister or my girlfriend. We had lunch because you've been on my mind and I needed someone to talk to."

"You're lying."

He looks at me seriously. "I love you, Charlie, I swear I do, but if you ever call me a liar again that's it. We through, do you understand me?"

I nod.

Since he's being real with me I decide to keep it one hundred with him. I'm trying to think of the right way to tell him the most important thing in my life and I decide to just say it, "Luke, I'm a man."

"What are you talking about?"

"I want you to know," I swallow, "that I'm a man, and that I've been lying to you."

"Charlie, I know you're a man," he laughs. "Why you coming at me all crazy and shit?"

I can't explain this moment. To discover that the one thing that I had been worrying about is dumb is not only life changing, but also it provided me with a major lesson. That you can never assume that you know what another person is thinking.

"What...how...I mean...I never told you."

"You don't remember seeing me in jail?" he asks me. "Because I remember you. You just made bail and I was coming inside. I remember thinking that the best part about being in there, was getting to see you. I figured you got away from me until I saw you at the bar. That's why I didn't want to stop chasing you on the street."

"Yes, I finally remembered you, but I looked a wretched mess in there and I thought...you...didn't remember me."

He chuckles. "Baby, I knew who you were, the moment I saw your face in that bar. I also know who you want to be, as far as the sex change. I overheard you fussing at Dixie in his room about it, one of the first times I went to your house. That's what made me hate him so much, because I don't like how he treats you."

"But you say you hate faggies."

"Let me explain something about me, I hate men who are gay, loud and dumb. That's my definition of faggies. I don't like them coming onto me and I'll put them in their place quick. That's why I got into a fight the night you met me. This faggy walked up to me and grabbed my ass, and I crushed him. With all that said, I'm still a gay man."

Tears pour down my face. "Luke, I feel like this is too good to be true. You accept me for me."

"Hold up, is that why you were telling me you couldn't have kids? Because you thought I thought you were a woman?"

"Yes," I say wiping my tears.

"Charlie, I don't want a woman."

"But I'm turning into one," I tell him.

"I ain't gonna lie, I've considered what you want, but I love you. And if that's how you want to live, I'll support you one hundred percent. If you would just be with me."

The rest of the night was filled with passion and lovemaking. And even though I was grateful for our bond, and the gift from God, there was still one last thing left to do.

CHAPTER TWENTY-NINE

Dixie

I woke up staring at the ceiling. I'm not going to lie, Charlie walking around the house without a care in the world pisses me off. I made a decision last night that today, I'm going to place an anonymous call to the police and tell them that he was responsible for the injection deaths of Gi-Gi and Fergie. I'm going to also tell them where they are buried.

When I try to sit up, I notice I can't. What the fuck is going on? WHY CAN'T I MOVE? I try again and again, and the only thing that motions on my body are my eyelids! I can't even open my mouth to talk. Why?

When Charlie walks into the room, I try to tell him I'm in trouble with my eyes.

"Good morning, Dixon," he says smiling. He's holding a red pill bottle in his hand.

I roll my eyes around rapidly trying to communicate with him but it doesn't work!

"I know what you're thinking right now. You're thinking, why can't I move my body. Well let me help you with that, you can't move because I have given you something to paralyze you." He shakes the pill bottle. "Courtesy of a dear friend of mine. And you will not move, unless I deem fit."

What the fuck does he mean?

"And let me tell you why I have done this to you," he continues. "I found out a lot about you that I didn't know before, a lot of things I don't like. I discovered that you are evil, probably the child of the devil. And because of it, I don't trust you."

He wipes the cascading curls out of his face, and I notice the diamond that is sitting on his finger. It looks like an engagement ring. I now know why he was screaming and jumping around last night. Luke proposed, and apparently he said yes. I'm devastated.

"I also know that you never had a heart murmur, Dixon. I know you been blackmailing me, and trying to make me feel bad to control me, and I know that will never happen again. I'm over you, Dixon. Those days are long gone, thanks to Sugar and my future husband," she flashes her ring and a tear rolls down my face.

How did he find these things out? I...I never meant to hurt him, I just wanted him to love me forever, and not leave me like Mr. Cram. If only I could talk to him, I would be able to explain everything. But I can't move. Why can't I move?

"To make sure that you will never hurt another person," he says walking up to me. "I am going to keep you paralyzed and unable to move. I don't know if it's going to be a few days, weeks or months. I do know that I won't stop the dosages until I can see that your eyes have changed.

"Now I don't want you to worry about your care, even though I still have my clients that I have to take care of. To ensure that you get cleaned and the like, I've hired a nurse who has no idea that I'm keeping you in this state. She'll help administer care when I'm out injecting my clients. Dixon, you have finally reaped what you sowed."

He lifts me up by my upper body, and my arms lazily fall behind his back. With a loud grunt he picks me up and places me into a wheel chair sitting beside the bed.

"This is going to be your new situation," he says pushing me toward the window. Every morning I'm going to come in and take you out of bed. And I'll push you to this window, so that you can see life passing you by. And when I'm ready, only when I'm ready," he continues whispering in my year, "your meds will stop." He runs his hand over my face.

SHAY HUNTER

"Don't be mad at me, Dixon, you always said you wanted me to take care of you, so here we are." He kisses me on my lumpy cheek, and walks out of the door.

As I stare out into the sunlight I know one thing above all. I don't care how long I have to live at some point in my life I'm going to pay Charlie back for this shit. And he will pay greatly too.

MEAN GIRLS ™

Mean Girls Magazine will offer women the opportunity to reach their full potential in all aspects of their lives, whether it be body, mind or soul. We believe that it's great to embrace your body no matter what shape or size. We believe that the color of your skin doesn't depict how beautiful you are inside or out. We believe it's good to be in tune with your sexuality, and not feel afraid to express yourself in the bedroom. We believe that your dream job may not necessarily involve a nine to five, and we are excited about showing you new and exciting opportunities to launch your career or business. We understand how it feels to be brokenhearted and excluded by those you love, and we support you by accepting you into a community of women just like you.

Mean Girls Magazine is not about being angry, bitter or hateful. It's about being your best, and de-

FOLLOW US:

Facebook: Mean Girls Magazine
Twitter: @meangirlsmag
Instagram: @meangirlsmag

Sign-up for updates on our website
www.meangirlsmagazine.com

EXTRA RAUNCHY
CHILDREN OF THE CATACOMBS

T. STYLES

NATIONAL BEST SELLING AUTHOR OF *RAUNCHY*

CARTEL PUBLICATIONS
(PRESENTS)

The Cartel Collection
Established in January 2008
We're growing stronger by the month!!!
www.thecartelpublications.com

Cartel Publications Order Form
Inmates ONLY get novels for $10.00 per book!

Titles		_Fee_
Shyt List	_____	$15.00
Shyt List 2	_____	$15.00
Pitbulls In A Skirt	_____	$15.00
Pitbulls In A Skirt 2	_____	$15.00
Pitbulls In A Skirt 3	_____	$15.00
Pitbulls In A Skirt 4	_____	$15.00
Victoria's Secret	_____	$15.00
Poison	_____	$15.00
Poison 2	_____	$15.00
Hell Razor Honeys	_____	$15.00
Hell Razor Honeys 2	_____	$15.00
A Hustler's Son 2	_____	$15.00
Black And Ugly As Ever	_____	$15.00
Year of The Crack Mom	_____	$15.00
The Face That Launched a Thousand Bullets		
	_____	$15.00
The Unusual Suspects	_____	$15.00
Miss Wayne & The Queens of DC		
	_____	$15.00
Year of The Crack Mom	_____	$15.00
Familia Divided	_____	$15.00
Shyt List III	_____	$15.00
Shyt List IV	_____	$15.00
Raunchy	_____	$15.00
Raunchy 2	_____	$15.00
Raunchy 3	_____	$15.00
Reversed	_____	$15.00
Quita's Dayscare Center	_____	$15.00
Quita's Dayscare Center 2	_____	$15.00
Shyt List V	_____	$15.00
Deadheads	_____	$15.00
Pretty Kings	_____	$15.00
Drunk & Hot Girls	_____	$15.00
Hersband Material	_____	$15.00
Upscale Kittens	_____	$15.00
Wake & Bake Boys	_____	$15.00
Young & Dumb	_____	$15.00
Tranny 911	_____	$15.00

Please add $4.00 per book for shipping and handling.
The Cartel Publications * P.O. Box 486 * Owings Mills * MD * 21117

Name: _____

Address:_____

City/State:_____

Contact # & Email:_____

Please allow 5-7 business days for delivery. The Cartel is not
responsible for prison orders rejected.

Personal Checks Are Not Accepted.

877
7864

CPSIA information can be obtained
at www.ICGtesting.com
Printed in the USA
LVOW08s1823021216
515532LV00001B/118/P